KING PENGU

REQUIEM FOR A WOMAN'S SOUL

Omar Rivabella is an Argentinian writer and journalist living
in New York. A strong advocate of human rights, he is the
author of several essays and short stories published in Latin
America. Between 1980 and 1983 he wrote three weekly
columns for *El Diario* in New York City. His articles have
also appeared in several American publications, including
Penthouse. Mr Rivabella's first novel, *El Cielo Está Sucio*, is
currently being translated into English. He is at present col-
laborating in a biography of the former light-heavyweight
champion José Torres.

OMAR RIVABELLA

———

REQUIEM FOR A WOMAN'S SOUL

TRANSLATED BY
PAUL RIVIERA AND OMAR RIVABELLA

A KING PENGUIN
PUBLISHED BY PENGUIN BOOKS

Penguin Books Ltd, Harmondsworth, Middlesex, England
Viking Penguin Inc., 40 West 23rd Street, New York, New York 10010, U.S.A.
Penguin Books Australia Ltd, Ringwood, Victoria, Australia
Penguin Books Canada Limited, 2801 John Street, Markham, Ontario, Canada L3R 1B4
Penguin Books (N.Z.) Ltd, 182–190 Wairau Road, Auckland 10, New Zealand

First published in the United States of America by Random House, Inc. 1986
Published in Penguin Books in the United States of America by arrangement with Random House, Inc. 1987
Published in Penguin Books in Great Britain 1987

Reproduced, printed and bound in Great Britain by
Hazell Watson & Viney Limited,
Member of the BPCC Group,
Aylesbury, Bucks

FOR JOSÉ TORRES

ACKNOWLEDGMENTS

I want to thank my editor Erroll McDonald for his valuable guidance, and the following people for their support: Jorge Saitta, Rudy Langlais, Juan Carlos Moran, Andrea de Urquiza, Rev. William Wipfler (American Council of Churches), John G. Healey (Amnesty International), Dr. Ruth Ann Turkel (American Psychiatric Association–Womens' Division), Dr. Silvia Olarte (Director, Inpatient Psychiatric Department, Lenox Hill Hospital), Reverend Onell A. Soto (Episcopal Church), and the members of AISC (Argentine Information Service Center).

I would also like to express my deepest appreciation to Dr. Orlando Garcia (Director, Richmond Behavioral Sciences Medical Center) and Reverend Carlos Mullins (Northeast Catholic Center) for their persistent encouragement, and to my daughter Adrianne for her help with the manuscript.

REQUIEM
FOR
A
WOMAN'S
SOUL

CHAPTER I

It was at the 7:00 A.M. mass that I saw her. She sat alone in the last row of pews, hugging a large cardboard box, that partially hid her face, on her lap.

It was the box that first caught my attention as I mounted the pulpit and briefly scanned the small nave, more out of habit than to find out which parishioners were present.

The eyes of the woman never left me as she fiercely held onto the box. I wondered if in her possession was a newborn infant.

During the mass I was obsessed with the woman and her cardboard box. Several times while praying I gazed furtively at her, searching for some clue to her identity. It had been six months since I had taken charge of this parish in this small town of less than one thousand inhabitants, and by now I had gotten to know almost everyone in town. But I had never seen this woman before—in church or on the street. I now had a sudden premonition that something secret and strange could erupt that morning.

At the end of the mass, as the congregation began to file out slowly, some waited at the foot of the pulpit to talk to me about private matters and were surprised when I did not descend the two steps to the floor. But all my attention was on that woman with the box, who stared straight ahead impassively despite the murmuring and the stares of the parishioners who passed her on the way out.

3

Her solitude amidst the empty pews, heightened by her extremely pale face, gave her an aura of sanctity.

The church was now empty.

The woman remained seated for another few minutes, as if she were making sure that no one would return. Then she placed her box on the bench next to her and emerged from behind the pew. As she took her first steps toward me, I noticed that she limped badly.

"Who are you?" I asked.

She didn't answer.

"How can I help you?"

She kept coming slowly toward me, her eyes focusing only on my lips.

"Are you all right? Who are you?" I stammered. As she came closer to me I realized that she was struggling to hear me.

"My name is Luisa. I became deaf over six months ago, Father," she said in a tone of despair that moved me to compassion.

"How can I help you?" I repeated slowly, exaggerating the movement of my lips. She read my lips carefully and paused.

"Susana sends you that," she said, pointing to the box in the pew.

Then she turned around and headed for the door.

"Who is Susana?" I shouted as she limped out of the church. She didn't look back.

"Who is Susana?" I shouted again, forgetting that she couldn't hear me.

I heard the sound of an engine outside the church and as I ran into the street I found myself enveloped by a cloud of dust raised by a compact car leaving the scene in a hurry.

Back inside the chapel, I went to the pew where the box lay. I stood there staring at it, uncertain about what to do next.

I approached the cardboard box cautiously. Slowly I slid

my fingers under it and strained to lift it. But I overestimated its weight and fell backwards, laughing nervously at my clumsiness.

I carried the box to my room in the parish house. The top was tightly secured by broad strips of adhesive tape. As I succeeded in opening the box, I was assaulted by an intense odor as of a mixture of urine and human excrement. Whatever lay at the bottom of the carton was covered by abundant wads of paper.

I recoiled, convinced that someone had played a bad practical joke on me. I grew afraid; I felt in danger. Before my transfer to this chapel a few months before to this desolate country village, Bishop Antonelli had warned me that my life might be threatened despite all our precautions. During the ten years I had been assigned to the Inmaculada Concepción *in the capital city, under Bishop Antonelli's jurisdiction, I had voiced strong criticism against the government's unjust treatment of the poor. I was a social worker. I had always thought, like a few other priests, that the church should be militant. Part of my admiration for Bishop Antonelli lay in the fact that he was one of the few in the high hierarchy who thought that our being politically submissive was a contradiction of our faith. He always encouraged us with his own involvements, and he often reassigned "outspoken" priests to protect them.*

In the small makeshift kitchen that Juanita, my housekeeper, had created for the few occasions on which I had dinner at the parish, I went through every drawer until I came across the rubber gloves Juanita wore to scrub the floors.

Back in my room, I opened the window to let the cool air of the morning flush out the lingering odor of the contents of the box.

Annoyed, I closed it, and kicked it into a corner, resolving to get rid of it the next day.

When I returned from mass the following morning, Juanita had cleaned my room, but the box was still in the corner.

"Why did you leave this trash here?" I called to her.

"It didn't look like trash to me, Father," she replied with an innocence that has always made me suspect her of being a rascal, a combination of candor and mischief I found disarming.

"There's writing on the pieces of paper, Father," she continued.

"Writing?"

"Yes, Father."

I unfolded one of the wads. "Go back to the kitchen," I said.

As soon as Juanita disappeared, I unfolded a second piece of the paper. Scribbled in such minute handwriting that I had to strain to read them, were three paragraphs of what seemed to be a diary. The entry was dated "January 18."

Today they led me hooded back to the same place. The muffled noises I heard as I walked up the metal stairs poured out like a flood when they opened the door. They ceased abruptly as soon as we entered.

"This nut here again?" asked the same voice that had yelled at me the time before. "You filthy seditious whore," he said, as he shoved a hard pointed object up my anus.

I struggled to control my impatience. Clumsily, I unfolded a few more pieces of paper. As I read them, I was overcome by nausea; my hands started to shake. An uncontrollable anguish swept over me, as when ten years before, I had read the first paragraphs of a letter from my sister telling me of the death of our mother.

I paced the room for a while trying to regain some calm. I then joined Juanita in the kitchen. I asked her to brew some coffee, and deliberately engaged her in small talk as a distraction.

Back in my room I grabbed a handful of the strips of paper and read. One hour later, I gave up reading and spent the rest of the day wandering along the muddy streets of the shanty town in the outskirts of the village, unable to chase away the ghost now haunting my life.

Then, one night, I picked up a few more of the little rolls with the absurd conviction that I was ready to make the self-sacrifice to face the challenge of exposing myself to whatever the notes would lead to. From that moment on, I set aside all my activities to decipher and organize the diary of an unknown woman.

CHAPTER II

For the next week I left my room only to say mass. My sermons were weak and my preaching unconvincing. I would head back to my room feeling ashamed at my inability to inspire. I would not even permit Juanita to enter.

She must have thought I was mad. The room looked like a dump. Scraps of paper were scattered all over the floor and on top of the night table. Some were pinned to the closet doors and on two wooden panels. Others which I was working on at the moment hung by clothespins from a wire I'd strung across the room, trying to decipher. Soon I realized that the length of the wire allowed me to lay out diary entries covering five days at a time. The work was not as disorganized as might appear at first glance, but it was complicated by the fact that after transcribing what I believed to be a complete entry, the resulting text would be incomprehensible. I would have to go

7

through the shreds of paper scattered on the floor until I found another one pertaining to the day in question. In other circumstances, perhaps I would have designed a more coherent plan, but I was consumed by anxiety. The complexity of the puzzle was irresistibly seductive.

CHAPTER III

January 6

There was banging at the door around 4:00 A.M., and when my father asked who it was, he heard a voice with authority identify itself as the police. Because my father is a doctor, and on previous occasions the police had asked him to treat seriously wounded "cases," he opened the door without hesitation. Six men dressed in army fatigues burst into the living room, knocking over everything in their way. Mama and I got to the living room in time to see one of the soldiers strike my father on the head with the butt of a gun, knocking him out. Two of the men pushed mama into the bedroom, and the others jumped on me. One of them covered my head with a thick hood while the other two held me as I tried to break free. It seems incredible that today, after so much has happened, I still vividly remember the sound of my fine linen nightgown being torn and the panic that came over me when, in that desperate fight, I swung my fist into the groin of the soldier who was trying to handcuff me.

They wrestled me to my feet and pushed me out of the

house. I stumbled over the unconscious body of my father. I heard one of them ask:

"What shall we do with the old folks?"

"The old man is going to sleep for a while," someone answered.

"And the old woman?"

There was some laughter. I fainted.

When I regained consciousness I found myself sprawled on the floor of a vehicle, a pair of boots pinning my body down. Someone asked:

"Shall we do it?" His partner answered no and from there on nobody spoke another word.

I could hear only the sound of the engine, and I thought that we must be moving along a road. Soon I realized, from the number of turns we made, that we were still in the city and that the surrounding silence was typical of early morning.

I have no idea how long we traveled, but when I was finally dragged out of the car, it was dark; no light penetrated the hood I was wearing. My captors' boots echoed as we walked down a corridor that led to a space where I could sense that I was in the company of other people. I don't know how long we were kept out in the open but I seem to remember periods of light and darkness, night turning to day. I was kept there for three or four days.

January 9?

During those days in the open I was blindfolded and fed only twice. Despite my pleas, I was not allowed to go to the bathroom. Neither were the others. By the second day the smell of urine and feces was unbearable.

January 10?

I sensed the special silence of dawn. I felt a blow to my left breast from the open hand of someone who had steathily approached me. Suddenly, I was suspended in midair as two men picked me up while laughing softly. One of them grabbed my feet while the other held me under my arms. I was carried back down the same corridor of days before and was dumped into a vehicle that seemed to be a jeep. They set off on another journey.

The three men riding with me in the back were disgusted by the stench of my body and viciously dug their boots into me all over (as revenge against whomever had given them this unpleasant assignment).

After almost an hour of traveling on bumpy dirt roads, a voice at some distance shouted, "Halt!" and the jeep came to a stop. I heard the sound of a barrier rising; we proceeded. Minutes later we stopped again. My three guards dismounted and two of them shoved me out and dragged me across a path of fine sharp gravel.

"Here's another seditious pig," said one of my custodians, as he kicked me in the pelvis.

"She looks like a good fuck," someone said.

"She stinks like hell."

"The boys will give her a bath." All of them exploded into laughter.

Two soldiers pulled me to my feet, fondling my breasts as they joked about the way I smelled. They pushed me through one door, then a second, which seemed to have glass panels. Another fifty paces and we stopped. I heard metallic noises and they shoved me onto a cot.

My left hand was shackled to the head of the bed.

I was left alone. I tried to remove the hood with my free hand, but it was tied securely at the back of my neck. Up to then, I had thought of nothing that was not immediate. Now, for the first time since my abduction, I thought of my parents, my fiancé and myself.

They gave me nothing to eat or drink. All that night I listened to the sounds of people being dragged from other cells. But the gloomiest of all was that I heard no human voices. I started sobbing.

January 12?
They led me to the bathroom twice and gave me a woolen skirt and a blouse stained with blood.

On one of my trips to the bathroom they removed the hood and I could see that the corridor had doors on each side that were identical to mine, iron doors with peepholes that could only be opened from the outside. My cell had a small window with iron bars and a fine wire mesh, and looked out onto a backyard.

January 13?
Today they opened my cell and asked me my name. I was surprised at my own voice. Besides sounding distorted inside the hood, I hadn't heard myself speak since I was kidnapped. The few times that I had attempted to talk they had silenced me with a beating.

A few hours later I heard the door open again and this time they asked my name *and* address. They asked my name three or four times during the day, and I welcomed those human voices that did not presage evil.

CHAPTER IV

The task wasn't getting any easier. The woman who had written the fragmented diary (I assume she is the "Susana" men-

tioned by the woman in the church) had been remarkably ingenious, but the ink had been exposed to moisture and entire paragraphs were completely blurred.

To further complicate things, in most cases an entry would be divided into three or four parts and on papers of different colors.

The April 17 entries, for example, consisted of a brief note on a match book, a longer one in the margin of a newspaper page, two lines on a piece of toilet paper and three entries on the back of the foil paper from a pack of cigarettes.

I would number the different strips from one day and hang them in order on the wire I had strung across the room.

At this stage of involvement, I realized that Susana had not kept to strict chronology in her notes and would often switch from past tense to present tense in a simple sentence.

Bearing in mind the circumstances under which this diary was written, I decided not to correct those inconsistencies, not to alter the document, thereby polishing off its credibility. For I am certain that this diary will become the subject of public controversy. So I've made up my mind to record every sensation, every emotion, all my experiences while I am engaged in my task. I will keep my own diary of the diary.

During this second week of insomnia I have transcribed the following:

CHAPTER V

January 14

I estimated that it was early evening when I started to hear the cell doors opening and prisoners being dragged through the corridor. I held my breath, fearing that my own door would be opened next.

I heard a key slip into the lock. I wet my skirt. They removed the handcuffs from my feet and unlocked the shackle that held me to the head of the bed. Once I got to my feet, they handcuffed my wrists behind my back.

"To the operating room!" I heard someone yell, and they started to shove me down the corridor. The gravel pierced my bare feet. Someone pushed my head down to prevent me from knocking myself unconscious on the door frame of the vehicle in which I was to be transported. They threw me on the floor in the back seat of the car and the soldiers who were seated rested their boots along my body.

They drove for over an hour.

Finally we stopped and I heard the sound of a radio-telephone. One of the soldiers in the front seat said something like "spider" and seconds later I heard heavy iron gates creaking open. They drove a little more and came to a halt. I was dragged out. I stumbled along for a considerable distance and was then forced to climb a steel staircase. They led me to a room where I heard the sound of glasses clinking (were people drinking?) and sensed the presence of several other persons. I felt eyes fixed on me and then I heard one of the men who brought me in say, "Have fun, boys."

I was taken down a narrow hallway and into a room. My handcuffs were removed. They stripped me and fondled me all over and then removed my hood.

In the room there was a table, a radio and a spotlight.

Ropes hung from the ceiling with butcher's hooks attached to the ends. Two naked women bound hand and foot were lying atop two dirty blood-stained metal bedframes.

There were three men in the chamber. One of them could easily have been taken for a dedicated teacher, as a result of his neat appearance and correct manners. The other two resembled characters taken out of a B-movie about gangsters and drugs. They addressed each other by nicknames. The one called "Nariz" had the classic look of a boxer; the other, "El Rengo," was short and dragged a lame leg as he walked. His small eyes and vicious stare provoked repulsion in me.

Nariz and El Rengo shoved me onto a bedframe and tied my hands and legs in the manner of the other two women.

They tied an electrical cord to one of my toes.

Standing nearby with hands bound behind their back were a man about thirty years old and a youngster about seventeen, each supervised by a guard. From their eyes, filled with hatred and anguish, I could tell that they were husbands or boyfriends or brothers of the two women.

When the torturers finished tying me up, they moved over to the older of the two women and the one who resembled a teacher applied an electrical wire to her, while Nariz and El Rengo looked on.

The elderly man began murmuring "Ana"... "Ana"... "Ana," as I heard spinechilling screams.

The torturer insistently asked the woman where a suspected terrorist arsenal was located but he didn't wait for an answer before again applying *la picana*, the mocking name they had given to their devilish electrical wire. Nariz broke off the torturing to go over and re-attach the electrical ground cable which had fallen off the toe of the other woman, a pretty girl of about sixteen.

El Rengo walked over to me and, with another electrical wire in his hand, exclaimed:

"And what about this other seditious little whore?"

My heart froze.

When he touched my head, my eyelids, my arms with the electrical wire, the shock shot through my body like lightning, altering my heartbeat. But when he touched my nipples, I felt not only pain but outrage.

He slid the wire slowly down my belly, while watching my various contortions. He circled my vagina several times with the wire and touched my clitoris with it.

Abruptly, he shoved the wire into my anus and a hideous pain led me to the verge of madness.

All the while he was also asking me about the terrorist arsenal; but he, too, gave me no chance to answer. At that point, the one who was torturing the older woman turned around to the girl and inserted the terminal into her vagina. Her body arched suddenly and violently and then she went into horrible convulsions. He waited for her to return to the original position and began touching her nipples with the electrical wire.

Ana and the two handcuffed men started screaming insults at the sadist; another guard turned up the radio to full volume.

"Who the hell is going to hear you?" he muttered, laughing.

The younger man started to cry, shouting over the loud music, "I love you, Cecilia, I love you."

"Now comes the best part," announced one of the torturers and immediately, one by one, guards and torturers began to rape and sodomize us. One of these beasts inserted a smooth, cylindrical stick into my anus, then said to me,

"You filthy whore, you'll enjoy it better when I give you the real thing later."

I lost consciousness.

January 15

I had a powerful desire to die.

January 16

All the day I lay hooded and motionless in the midst of a thick darkness. Solitude became something tangible. I can almost touch my loneliness. I am afraid *they* have succeeded in creating a feeling of total isolation. Lack of stimulus makes my thoughts more vivid. I try hard not to remember. Most of the time it is unavoidable. When I think about Mama or Papa I feel like an orphan.

January 17

I haven't had anything to eat for the last two days. The physical pain has been receding. They have twice taken me to the bathroom but my urine was pure blood. All day long I have been thinking of Nestor . . .

CHAPTER VI

I was set adrift by a disturbing suspicion. I dropped the note on the desk.

I walked back and forth several times between the window

*and the desk. I had the feeling that I knew Nestor. More
troubling yet, I had the feeling that I knew Susana.*

*I kept pacing back and forth until I gathered enough cour-
age to pick up the small piece of paper. My eyes jumped over
the lines.*

I read on.

". . . All day long I have been thinking of Nestor . . . and
his caresses. Even though we were engaged, I always told
him that he had to be patient. I used to tell him jokingly
that if he didn't behave I would tell Father Antonio."

*The reference to me—to my name written in that tiny uneven
handwriting—numbed my senses. It took a while for me to
realize who Susana was. Suddenly my legs seemed unable to
support the weight of my body. I lay down in bed. I read the
note once more. I had been Susana's family priest in my
previous parish.*

*I was there when she started worrying about her pimples
and when at thirteen she came to church, crying, to confide
her first romantic disappointment in me. I saw her as she
grew. I was there when she received her Bachelor's degree
from the Instituto de la Misericordia.*

*One day, I met Nestor. She brought him to church and
introduced me as "the priest who will marry us."*

*I liked him instantly. He was a handsome medical student,
of a new generation that is trying to change things without
resorting to extremism. He started attending the church of the
Inmaculada Concepción. After a while, it wasn't difficult to
persuade him to help me in the shanty towns around the city.
The imaginative Nestor gathered a few friends from medical
school and created a voluntary service under the somewhat
pompous name of Inmaculada Concepción Health Program.*

*Susana ran most of the time between hovels looking for
children with high fever or running noses, or assisted Nestor
when he had to treat more serious cases. She was also in
charge of administering our lean "budget" consisting mostly*

of goods, not money, donated by merchants from the more affluent areas.

I recall the last time I saw them as if it happened an instant ago. Susana, Nestor and I were having lunch in a ramshackle hut in a very poor section of the city.

The day before Nestor had come with me to the bedside of a dying child, and while I administered the extremaunción, I had seen him looking the other way to hide his tears. I remember thinking that he was going to be a good doctor. It takes time to get used to misery.

All morning on that last day Nestor had treated infections while Susana comforted weary mothers who had more children than they could feed. At lunch in the humble dwelling of a poor family, they were sporting the engagement rings that I had blessed at the home of Susana's parents during a simple ceremony. I remember joking about a twinkling from Susana's ring as she put it on her finger.

Since learning of Susana's identity, my attitude toward the diary that I have been deciphering has changed in a way I can't define. I am neglecting my pastoral duties even more. For a couple of days I tried to resume the routine of catechism; I visited the dispensary and made daily rounds through the mud-and-cardboard shanties that the new municipal chief, an army captain serving as the junta's man, had hidden by a brick wall representing his most important contribution to the town's progress.

My negligence is becoming evident and already the parishioners are whispering that I am "turning lazy." I suspended the nine o'clock mass and eliminated the weekly dinner with the Ladies for Catholic Action.

A few days ago I received a letter from Bishop Ovando inquiring about my health. He has never been pleased to have me under his jurisdiction. I have been more or less an annoyance he has tolerated out of respect for Monsignor Antonelli.

One day the soft-spoken patriarch, Monsignor Antonelli, respected more for the man he was than for his ecclesiastic rank, said to me:

> *"Antonio, I have lost part of my flock, the best part I should say, at the hands of those intoxicated with power. We are living through times in which it is necessary to reason whether it is better to rescue the lamb from the wolf than to use all the power of the spear. I think, Antonio, I must hide you for a while within the foliage of our Mother Church."*
> *"Why?"*
> *"Your work is not well regarded."*

Monsignor Antonelli went on to say that my work with the poor had been considered by the regime as indoctrination in dangerous ideologies. I explained to him that I was only trying to help those people, inspiring them with the faith necessary to keep them from renouncing God in the face of the inhuman conditions in which they were forced to live. Monsignor Antonelli said that in other times priests like me were called missionaries.

A great sadness overcame me when I was transferred to Monsignor Ovando, who was more than one thousand kilometers away. A document released by the prelate had identified him as a bishop in favor of passivity towards repression.

Yet, I didn't oppose the transfer. Monsignor Antonelli had never made an arbitrary decision since I had known him and it was obvious that he knew a great deal more than what he cared to tell me about the danger I was in.

So it was that I replaced old Father Ramiro in this remote town, surrounded by treacherous mountains and beautiful landscapes that cannot conceal its poverty.

I am sure that Monsignor Ovando has already contacted the patriarch about the strange behavior of his protégé and that worries me. But at the same time, I am just as sure that Monsignor Antonelli would condone my state of mind if he knew the underlying reasons. Someday he will.

I have lived this week in a quasi-monastic state, eating very little. Every morning Juanita waits for me at my door and actually forces me to eat a little something before going to the 7:00 A.M. mass. My physical condition grows weaker, as my obsession with the diary grows stronger. I am beset by ferocious headaches and dizziness. Still, at the end of this week I have transcribed more entries.

CHAPTER VII

January 18

Today they led me hooded back to the same place.

The muffled noises I heard as I walked up the metal stairs poured out like a flood when they opened the door. They ceased abruptly as soon as we entered. "This nut here again?" asked the same voice that had yelled at me the time before. "You filthy seditious whore," he said, as he shoved a hard pointed object up my anus.

"Was she good to you, Nariz?" asked one of the men who brought me back. Laughter came from the other end of the room as someone else remarked, "It was the first time Nariz had a virgin."

The laughter built as he replied, "The filthy slut fainted. It was like fucking a corpse."

When they removed the hood I saw that Ana was there,

too, but not the young girl called Cecilia. Neither were the two young men. But there was another woman on the center bedframe. She must have been about twenty-five. She was tied up in a spread-eagle position and had bluish lumps all over her body. A man standing near her with an electrical wire in his hand asked the other guards for Cecilia's whereabouts.

"She was still in very good fucking condition so we decided to give her to the lieutenant as a present," responded one of my guards.

For the first time, they asked me if I knew Silvia Molinari.

January 19

My custodians were more vicious than ever during this trip to the torture chamber. Ana was already there along with the new girl I had met the previous day. There was also a man in uniform I had never seen before, whom everybody addressed reverentially as "the lieutenant."

"So, you know Silvia?" he said as soon as they removed my hood.

"Yes."

"Where is she?"

"I don't know."

The lieutenant punched me hard in my stomach and as I doubled over he ordered the men to undress me. They tied me up and at a signal from the lieutenant the ones that were torturing the other women started to give me electrical shocks while the lieutenant demanded to know, "Where is Silvia? . . . Where is she?"

My not knowing only infuriated him and he ordered the voltage increased.

A third torturer was instructed to apply electricity to my gums. I lost consciousness. As I regained consciousness, I became aware of a man trying to resuscitate me, and he relaxed when I opened my eyes.

January 20

The lieutenant was there again. So was Ana and the other woman. This time I noticed with great surprise that the other woman was smiling and looked at me with a friendly expression, which I thought was peculiar. As she received the electric shocks, her body arched but she kept smiling in absolute silence.

The lieutenant came over to where I lay and again asked me about Silvia, striking me with a whip almost immediately. He grabbed a pair of headphones he had requested and placed them over my ears. The steady high-pitched sound drove me into unconsciousness at once.

When I opened my eyes later, the lieutenant was asking me not only about Silvia but also about her boyfriend. He turned red with fury when I answered "I don't know." Once again, he savagely struck me, then shoved the hilt of his whip into my anus. As I was passing out, I saw him throw the whip to a subordinate, ordering him to "wash it off."

January 22

I heard the door of the cell adjoining mine opening; I heard voices, punches thrown, but no cries, no wailing.

I imagined the woman in that cell smiling and it occurred to me that maybe she was one of those persons who had the ability to attain, at will, a hypnotic state that can block pain from the nervous system.

I had once heard of a pianist who while being tortured had played Bach in his head. And a surgeon who imagined anesthetizing the parts of his body being touched by the electric wires. What was the resource of the girl in the next cell? What did she imagine?

The beating lasted for about another twenty minutes. There were no cries.

January 26

I had not been led to the house of torture for four days. I would later learn from Alicia that such respites were the result of too many "clients" on their hands.

There were different guard shifts and different attitudes among the guards. Some would permit me to remain without the hood and handcuffs. There was a guard who even looked at me with compassion, though he never spoke.

Another guard, however, would shackle my hands and feet to the bed and never took me to the bathroom. As much as I tried not to, I would invariably soil myself. This would infuriate him and, after cursing me, he would train a cold hose on me while I was shackled to the cot. The cells appeared to have been designed for events of this nature since in the floor there was a hole covered with a wire mesh to drain the water and excrement.

Still another guard entered the cell only to fondle me. He would whisper obscenities in my ear and, while fondling me, threaten to kill me if I resisted him. "Son of a bitch, son of a bitch," I repeated to myself.

"Son of a bitch." One day the words escaped.

The pervert only laughed. Shortly after, I felt warm slime sliding down between my breasts. Diligently, he wiped me clean, retied my hood and left.

January 27

Around midnight I was taken out of the cell and led to a vehicle. I was thrown on top of another woman, who groaned. As I tried to shift my weight off her one of the guards became aware of what I was doing and started stomping all over me.

Once at the torture house, they removed our hoods and I discovered that my traveling companion was the girl with the smiling face. I tried to convey with a glance how sorry

I was at having trampled her in the car. She gave back such a tender look.

We were stripped and shackled on two metal bedframes. On the third one was a woman who was about seven months pregnant. Standing near my bed and under the custody of two guards was a rather young man whose hands were hand-cuffed behind him.

"Watch, so you'll learn," one of the torturers ordered. Then he began applying the *picana* to the woman's vagina. The other torturer did likewise, intermittently touching her nipples with another live wire.

When the young man turned his head away, unable to watch, one of the guards hit him in the temple with the butt of his gun and yelled:

"Look how your wife is suffering because of you, you guerilla son of a bitch!"

A grey-haired man addressed respectfully by his nick-name, "Dr. Mengele," wearing a white blazer and sporting a stethoscope around his neck, monitored her vital signs as she was being tortured. Suddenly he seemed to be annoyed.

"You beasts!" he shouted.

The torturers stepped back.

"What is it, Doctor?" asked one of them.

Without comment "Dr. Mengele" leaned over the woman and dried the tears from her face. He asked her in a com-passionate voice how she felt. All the while he attached a spoon to wires handed him by one of the torturers. He in-serted the spoon into the woman's vagina, the burst of elec-tricity no doubt shocking her fetus. The other two torturers closely observed the scene. At a signal from Dr. Mengele, one of them went to the control panel and increased the voltage.

The young woman began hemorrhaging. Spasms ripped through the woman's body. She lay motionless.

Mengele examined her with a mixture of annoyance and resignation, then remarked:

"We overdid it again."

The young man rushed over to the bedframe where his wife's body lay still, shouting:

"Murderers!"

He was silenced by a gunshot to the back of the neck by one of his custodians. He fell on top of me, spurting blood. One of his eyes had been blown out of its socket.

I felt something warm oozing down my legs; I fainted.

When I came to, the torturer and Doctor Mengele were amiably discussing who was to blame for what had happened. Mengele was giving intricate explanations of the effects of electric discharges on the coronary arteries.

The dead couple had been removed. The torturers seemed bored. One of them came over to my bed and remarked:

"This nut conveniently fainted."

Next they moved to the girl with the friendly eyes. I imagined her still smiling. Then they resumed working on me. I tried thinking of Bach, but to no avail. I looked forward to blacking out.

January 30

In the dark solitude of my cell, in which I had remained for almost three days, I began thinking about what life had been like before the sixth of January.

My parents had been maybe a little overprotective; they had always taken every opportunity to show how much they cared for me. Nestor was in love with me, and we were to be married on the twentieth of June. I was to have been graduated from college with a degree in literature in two years. I often imagined the diploma which my mother would hang prominently beside my typewriting certificate, and my citation from the music academy.

Here, under these circumstances, I have invented some games to keep from going mad. I shape figures out of the tripe I save from the rancid sandwiches they give me at times. I christen one particular fly out of a swarm attracted by the smell of urine and excrement and follow its flight among the others. Despite the danger of being caught and punished I often spend considerable time near the drainage hole where the flies concentrate most and with a swipe of the hand try to trap one or two. I feed a long-legged spider that has woven its web in one of the corners of the cell.

The spider seemed to recognize me, because as soon as I came near, it would rush to the center of the web where I normally deposited the flies I had trapped. I notice how the spider renders its prey defenseless, and I hope it is not one of the flies I have christened.

During the past three days the guard who keeps me hand-cuffed and hooded has been on duty. I have not been able to play. I am left to my recollections.

My resentment against Silvia is mounting.

January 31
In a room in the same building I was forced to stand facing a wall.

A hoarse voice behind me asked my name and place of birth.

"Do you know Silvia Molinari?" he asked.

"Yes," I answered.

"Where is she?"

"I don't know."

"Were you friends?"

"Only acquaintances."

"Do you know why you are here?"

"No."

"For being another pawn of the anarchic terrorism that is trying to undermine the foundations of our democracy."

"I am not . . ."

"Shut up," shouted my interrogator. "In this dirty war the Armed Forces are determined to shed every drop of blood to preserve the Christian values of the West."

"But I am not . . ."

"Shut up," he screamed at me again.

"Answer me. Do you hate the Armed Forces?"

I didn't answer. There was a prolonged silence.

"Do you know Silvia Molinari?" he started again.

"Yes."

"Where is she?"

"I don't know."

"Were you friends?"

"Just acquaintances."

"When did you see her for the last time?"

"The day she gave me letters from her boyfriend."

"Do you know her boyfriend?"

"No."

My interrogator walked away.

From the clicking of the boot heels, I assumed he was a high ranking army officer.

I was kept standing in the same spot for almost three hours. Finally, without further questions, I was returned to my cell. Lying on the cot that night I tried to reconstruct my last meeting with Silvia.

Nestor had found a small apartment near the Faculty of Medicine. My father offered to pay for a painter. Nestor politely refused and painted it himself during nights and weekends. Already we bought furniture on credit, and on the day that it was being delivered I was supposed to stop by the apartment after trying on my wedding dress.

At the corner, I met Silvia and we walked leisurely the six blocks to the dressmaker. She told me she had been writing to her childhood sweetheart who was a private in the Army. She was being especially secretive since her mother had found his letters from him to her and disapproved of their relationship. I then noticed the bundle of letters she was carrying.

She asked me to hold onto them for her.

After two years of knowing Silvia I had developed a certain liking for her, though we weren't really close friends and our relationship had been limited to casual chats at a nearby café after classes, and always in the presence of other students.

Leaving the dressmaker, I went to the apartment and placed the letters in the bottom drawer of the night table. I remember the soft perfume on the pink ribbon with which they were tied.

That night I told Nestor about the letters and he made some jokes about my romantic attitude. He also smiled. Nestor always understood.

February 1
Shackled to the bedframe, I spent all day looking at the spider running back and forth from one end of the web to the other. Then the day after the last encounter with Silvia forced its way into my mind.

It was late in the afternoon of January 5 when I finished ironing the curtains that I would hang in our apartment. I left home with the bundle of drapes and a new set of ballpoint pens that I bought as a present for Nestor. I wanted to place them—as is traditional on the eve of the Epiphany—inside the shoes Nestor bought especially for the wedding, which he kept in the bedroom closet of the apartment.

The building superintendent was mopping the floor in the lobby as I came in, and didn't answer my greeting. He didn't lift his eyes from what he was doing, which I thought strange.

I went up to the third floor thinking about his discourtesy. As I opened the door to our apartment I was struck by total disarray. The upholstery had been slashed and the stuffing was lying all about the floor. The legs of the coffee table had been broken and shattered glass was everywhere. The doors on the china cabinet had been pulled off their hinges, and porcelain was missing. Gone also was the television set and the typewriter. The bedroom clock was no longer there, and the closet where Nestor had stored his souvenirs was ransacked. The drawers from the night tables were overturned on the boxspring; the mattress was on the floor, cut from one end to the other.

I rushed down to the lobby to the superintendent.

"We have been robbed! We have been robbed!" I said in desperation.

He raised his eyes from the rag he was sliding in circles over the tiles, but didn't stop working.

"In this building we don't want people with problems," he said in a reproachful tone.

"What do you mean?"

"You know what I mean."

"No, I don't," I answered, irritated.

"They came last night."

"Who are they?"

"The militia."

"What militia?"

The man stood up.

"I can't say another word," he uttered frightfully.

I grabbed him by the arm.

"What militia?" I repeated.

"The men from the Army," he said as he tried to break free from me. I held onto him but felt pity as I recognized the terror on his face.

"Please, lady," he begged. "I don't want to get involved; I have a family. They told me not to talk to you. Don't ask me anything, leave me alone." He verged on panic.

I ran back home in madness. I called Nestor but he wasn't

home. His mother told me he had an emergency call; there had been an attempted coup at a military base, with many casualties.

I called Father Antonio and was told he had to travel to the interior of the country and they didn't know when he would be back. I kept calling Nestor until very late that night but his mother had no news.

Then came January 6.

CHAPTER VIII

Today I received another letter from Bishop Ovando. He begs me to come down to the city to discuss the creation of a home for the aged.

This town needs an old people's home like it needs a nuclear holocaust. The few remaining elderly are living first class with their children and play bochas *nine hours a day on any flat piece of ground they can find.*

Bishop Ovando doesn't know this, but he had to imagine something to lure me to his side so as to scold me about my work.

I wrote back, saying that because of my exhaustive efforts in developing various charity projects, I had to humbly ask for a postponement of our conversation until such works were fully organized. I suspected that he wouldn't believe this, but I wanted to buy some extra time to conclude my work on the diary.

I haven't made much progress this week. I have been suf-

fering from insomnia. I am awakened by hallucinations and nightmares when I do manage to fall asleep—nightmares about Susana.

I wake up howling in terror and drenched in sweat. Twice I have awakened to Juanita pounding on my door, begging me to tell her what is wrong. The next morning, I would give her a confusing theological explanation of my dreams, which she would accept on faith. I asked her to keep this our little secret, but now I realize that that was a mistake, for that very afternoon Dr. Ortiz came around inquiring about my health. I have also fallen under the suspicion of the storeowner at La Central and one of the Ladies of Catholic Action who had recommended Juanita to me when I first came to take charge of the parish.

My obsession with the diary is complete.

CHAPTER IX

February 2

When they removed the hood in the torture chamber I could see a young girl, whose frail body hung from the butcher's hook. One of the guards operated a pulley that raised and lowered the girl's body.

One of the three torturers stood directly in front of her body. All I could see were his broad shoulders, which hid the meager body of the girl. Her body swung violently and hit the wall, and there was a hideous sound of bone crushing.

"Where is Avila?" the torturer asked as the body swung

back towards him like a dummy in an experiment. The girl's eyes were fixed.

"Avila, where is he?" the man repeated.

The girl spat in his face; she delivered a macabre laugh. The torturer wiped the spittle from his cheek.

"God damned little whore," he said, punching her in the stomach.

The door was pushed open and the lieutenant entered the room.

They spoke but I didn't understand. The lieutenant then signaled the man operating the ropes to raise the girl higher still.

Another signal from the lieutenant, and the other two torturers left the room and returned with several empty bottles which they smashed on the floor under the girl's feet.

At a nod from the lieutenant, the man in charge of the ropes began to lower the girl. The woman tried to raise her legs to avoid the broken glass but could only control the right one.

"What happened?" the lieutenant asked the man beside him.

"She hit the wall," he answered smiling.

The lieutenant ordered the man pulling the ropes not to lower the woman any further, and approached her, wiping the tears from her face.

"I am going to send you to the hospital for treatment," he told her tenderly.

She just stared at him.

"Where is Avila?" he inquired again.

There was no reply.

"Where is Avila?" he insisted in a soft, patient tone.

She remained silent. The lieutenant kicked broken glass out of the way and positioned himself squarely in front of her. He spread his hands, ready to clap her ears and asked again:

"Where is Avila?"

Without waiting for an answer, he struck her ears with his palms.

She let out a short, loud scream. She lost consciousness. The lieutenant kept at it, then gave some additional instructions and left. Shortly after, "Dr. Mengele" stepped in and, with a ball of cotton, wiped away the blood running out of the girl's ears.

February 3

Today one of the torturers began to amuse himself by shamelessly caressing my body, while delivering a lecture about "foreign and dangerous ideologies." He also made reference to the "important function" he was undertaking "in the official quest for the eradication of such."

He then softened his voice and began telling me about his daughter who was my age. He said he wanted her to become a dentist, since it was a well paying career, but "she turned out to be too much of a romantic dreamer" and, like me, had chosen to study literature.

"Well," he said, "what can you do? These youngsters of today! Do you want me to bring you some of the foolish things she writes tomorrow?"

The other torturer listened in on the conversation and was starting to say something about the grades his younger son had gotten at the Polytechnic when the lieutenant showed up.

"Did you see what happened yesterday to the other woman for refusing to answer my questions?" he asked, standing by my bed.

"From now on she'll be called "Deaf Luisa," remarked one of the torturers.

The lieutenant burst out laughing and the two men joined him. He started asking me the same questions over and over. Soon he became bored and left. Back in my cell that night

I heard for the first time the yapping of a puppy under the window. It reminded me of my dog Rulito which Nestor had given to me as a present. The noise sounded exactly like the piteous howling that had kept the entire family up every night during Rulito's first week at home. I tried to hold back my tears but the terrifying feeling of sudden and total abandonment to the will and the ways of evil was overwhelming. I dreamt of the ghostly image of "Dr. Mengele" tenderly wiping the blood from Luisa's ears over and over. It wasn't entirely a bad dream.

February 4
I miss my father as much as I miss my mother. I have never realized I love him so much. At times I was overwhelmed by the feverish desire to be hugged by him as when I was a child. I am sure he has never witnessed torture. I am sure. He would never have allowed a human being to be tortured in his presence. I am sure.

February 5
They came to pick me up on a different schedule today. I know because on the previous occasions I could sense the quiet of the late night or of the early morning hours. Today, however, I was able to sense in the streets the agitation of daily life.

As they removed my hood, I saw a naked man, also hooded, on one bed and a pregnant woman on another.

I blushed at the sight of the man's nakedness. I was tied down to the bed in the middle and I turned my head as much as I could toward the bed where the woman lay. I was struck by her extraordinary beauty. I smiled at her, I hoped we gave each other courage.

Our captors were applying electrical shocks to the man while asking him something about his contacts in a terrorist organization, called something or other. The man refused to give any answers and his interrogator ordered the voltage increased.

I kept my eyes closed hearing only a groan. The interrogator repeated his question and again the man remained silent.

"Leave him to me," said another torturer, approaching the bed with a plastic tray in his hands.

"Shouldn't they watch?" asked the interrogator who had failed to obtain any answers.

"Of ̩ourse, Nariz, of course."

Two men came over and turned our heads in the direction of the scene.

"Don't close your eyes or I will have to leave a couple of nasty scars on that lovely face of yours, my dear Alicia," said the man holding Alicia's head.

He pressed the blade of a short knife to her throat and pulled her up by the hair.

"The same for you," muttered the man who was forcing me to look at the naked body of the hooded man.

The man who had taken charge of the interrogation picked up a razor blade from the tray and began carving out small squares of flesh from the arms of the man screaming and writhing. During one of his contortions the razor penetrated his skin deep enough to sever an artery. Blood spurted into the face of the torturer and spattered all of us.

When I regained consciousness, the tortured man had been removed from the room and Alicia was unconscious. As soon as I opened my eyes, the torturer who had talked to me the previous day about his daughter's poems stood by my bed with a sheet of paper in his hand.

"This one woke up," he said to the others.

I was shaking all over.

"How many are there in your unit?" he asked, reading from the sheet of paper.

Before I could answer I received a shock to my gums.

35

"In what area do you operate?" he asked again.

"What *cuadros* do you have?" he demanded.

None of this meant anything to me. Even if it had it would have made no difference to them because they weren't looking for answers that day. The man in charge of reading the questions asked for a break and took another sheet of paper from his back pocket.

"These are my daughter's poems," he said to me proudly, "I'll put them in the pocket of your skirt. Tell me tomorrow if you like them."

In the meantime, Alicia came to, and they moved over to her bed.

One of the torturers passed the *picana* over the pregnant woman's stomach and began singing in a babyish voice:

"Look how Juancito is moving . . . look how Juancito is moving."

The others joined in chorus and clapped, while occasionally feeling the woman's abdomen to see if the fetus was twitching.

"Cut the shit!" the lieutenant yelled as he entered the room.

The torturers stared in surprise at the officer, who summoned them to a far corner of the room. There was muttering among them and shortly after we were led back to our cells.

Back in my cell, I heard again the piteous yelping of a puppy.

CHAPTER X

Last night I woke up looking instinctively for blood around me and, noticing a dark spot on my pillow, I touched it, only to feel the wetness of my own perspiration.

As I turned over to check the time on the alarm clock on the night table, I felt such a sharp pain in my leg. I groped along it to be sure it wasn't fractured. I began to weep.

It is all madness. Two priests at a remote parish in the interior of the country were assassinated and their bishop suggested in his elegy that the mission of the Church should be strictly of an evangelistic nature. He added a few words regarding the "law and order of our Armed Forces" and "ideologies incompatible with the doctrine of our Lord Jesus Christ." He also said something about being "under the protection of God."

Everything was carefully worded, but in essence, it was a warning to those of us who believe that part of our clerical duty is to take action to help those in need. To give food to the poor is to be a subversive. To march with mothers whose sons have disappeared is to support the enemies of the government.

At the next seven o'clock mass, I sprinkled my sermon with a few references to corruption in the country. I mentioned repression.

The parishioners became restless. When I used the word

"disappeared," everyone turned to look at the police com- missioner and the army captain.

The two men looked at me impassively and when the mass was over they approached me.

With the exception of Rosa Urquia and another woman with a face full of wrinkles whom I had only seen on my rounds through the impoverished neighborhood at the edge of town, everybody else left church in a hurry.

The captain and the police commissioner stared at the women, ordering them with their eyes to leave, but neither budged from the pew.

"My wife and I would be deeply honored if you would join us for supper tomorrow," the captain said to me.

"It would be a pleasure," I answered, managing a smile, "but I already have accepted an invitation from Rosa." I pointed to the woman.

Rosa looked surprised. I had hardly exchanged greetings with her when she came to mass, and all I knew about her was that she was a teacher and had been suspended because of her husband's labor union activities.

"How about the following day," said the captain, trying to conceal his displeasure.

"Fine," I replied courteously.

Both men ignored the women as they walked out in silence.

I apologized to Rosa for using her but I needed that day and the following one to finish some work. She looked dis- appointed.

"Am I too poor to have you at my table, Father?" she asked. Her cleverness was clear. I promised her a visit.

Back in my room, I eagerly transcribed the following:

CHAPTER XI

February 6

The first guard to enter my cell during what I believe to be the night hours was the pervert who, after his usual fondling and obscenities, ejaculated again all over my breasts.

"So that you will know that I am not all bad, I brought you a present," he said affectionately while wiping semen off my chest.

Before leaving, he placed a bread roll in my left hand and pressed my fingers closed around it.

As soon as the lock clicked I dropped the roll. I again had to endure many hours of immovability and darkness.

The next guard shift to come on duty were the cleaners. They washed the room with a cold water hose, then trained it on me. After the initial shock of the coldness, I was grateful for the bath. They untied me, took off the hood and left.

I had discovered that by placing my ear against the bed-frame, I could tell by the intensity of the vibrations when the guards were in the corridor. When I felt reasonably safe, I carefully tried to get up from the bed. My legs were so numb I could barely stand. When I managed to take a few steps in the cell I was flooded by an ineffable feeling of freedom.

When I was certain that the guards in the corridor had moved away from my cell in the direction of the bathroom, I looked for the bread roll. I found it, now a pulpy mess over the drainage hole. I brushed off the flies that were feasting on it and squeezed it as if it were a sponge. I ate what was left of the sticky mess with definite delight. My hunger pangs disappeared.

I was almost feeling well when I heard moaning in the backyard.

Through the bars of the tiny window of the cell, I saw a man tied to a post in the center of the yard. Near him was another man bound to the ground by stakes.

Both were naked and their bodies were covered with large bruises. The sun was shining bright and I guessed that the two men must have been there since early morning, for the one on the ground had sunburn blisters.

Nearby, a guard amused himself by spitting watermelon seeds.

The one shackled to the post stared desperately at the piece of watermelon. He would follow the flight of each seed with his eyes until it landed over the body of the one on the ground. Aware of this, the guard would spit the next seed higher in the air imitating the sound of a plane as it descended the ground.

I did not hear my cell door being opened. Before I realized it, two guards were standing at my side. One of them kicked me in the back with such force that I slammed into the wall and fell to the floor.

They chained me to the cot and beat me until I fainted. When I woke up, my hood was on; I could still hear what I took to be a puppy outside.

February 7

As they took me to the bathroom I again saw those kind eyes staring at me through the peephole of the adjoining cell.

Back in my cell I discovered that the peephole on my door

had been shut and, after complying for a while with the order to remain on the cot, I stole to the window.

There was a spot of blood in the courtyard where yesterday one of the men had been staked to the ground. The other man was still chained to the post. He looked thinner now, and he, too, was covered with blisters.

A German shepherd came close to him, growling and snarling, while a voice in the background commanded the animal to be still. Although I knew it was impossible for anyone to see me, I backed away from the window. Soon two men, dressed in civilian clothes but wearing identical pairs of black boots, neared the center post.

They were discussing something between them. The younger one was unchaining the prisoner. I couldn't hear what they were saying. The younger one tied a rope around the waist of the captive, then made him walk until the rope, which was held by the man with the whip, became taut.

"Run!" he commanded the prisoner with such a violent shove that the man fell down, raising a cloud of dust.

"Run!" he yelled again, pulling him up by the hair.

The man staggered a few steps.

"Faster!" shouted the one with the whip. The man quickened his pace.

The man with the whip cracked it over the back of the prisoner. His companion viciously kicked the man as he went by him in circles. The man was whipped so viciously he started to bleed.

February 8

When the hood was removed from my head, I found myself in a room larger than the one I had known. In the center there was something like an indoor pool for children, only deeper. A pulley hung from the ceiling; a butcher's hook was attached to the rope. Against the wall was a set of racks to which two men were tied, facing the wall.

I was pushed over to them and ordered to sit beside the older one, who couldn't have been more than thirty years old. He had deep circles under his eyes and a sad but cool expression on his face. I felt affection for him; I'm not sure why.

A set of heavy shackles were affixed to his ankles and the guard helped him to stand and made him walk. The guard tripped him and he fell to the concrete floor but did not make a sound. Soon, another torturer used the butcher's hook to hoist the man by his leg irons like a side of beef.

The man was suspended over the water tank and the torturers waited until he stopped swinging to start interrogating him about an attack on some military quarters. The man remained silent. Fifteen to twenty minutes later, his face turned red from blood rushing to it.

The torturer who seemed to be in control of the inquiry signalled the operator of the pulley who started to lower the body slowly. The man contracted all his muscles in an effort to delay immersion. The torturer let the rope slip between his fingers and the man's head slipped deep into the water.

He kicked furiously while drowning. When his movements seemed to stop, the one in charge signalled again and the man was raised. As his head came out of the water, he was again asked about the attack on the military installations but again he said nothing.

The man underwent this routine until he lost every sign of life. He was then lowered to the ground and one of the torturers left the room and returned with a distinguished looking man who had a stethoscope dangling from his neck.

He examined the victim as if bored.

"That's all for today," he said very casually. The body was dragged out of the room.

Everyone else left, with the exception of one guard who was reading a magazine. Occasionally, he paused to glance at me and the younger prisoner beside me. I lost control of my bowel movement.

"To the tub!" ordered the chief as he reentered the room.

Two men grabbed me and dumped me into the cold water tank. My hands and feet bound by shackles, I sank to the bottom and, after what seemed an eternity, I was pulled by the hair back to the surface.

"Now she's spotless clean," one of the men remarked.

"Hook her up!"

As I regained consciousness back in my cell, hooded and bound to the bed, I tossed from side to side, almost as if to convince myself that I was still alive. I heard again the yelping of Rulito. I knew it was Rulito.

CHAPTER XII

Again I woke up with a brutal headache. During mass I realized that attendance had dropped and the few who had gathered enough courage to come to worship God looked at me strangely.

Absent were the captain and the police commissioner. Rosa and the woman with the face full of wrinkles were seated in their usual places. Around them, there were several people from the poor neighborhood whom I had never seen in church before.

The pathetic group of women in torn clothing and the un-shaved men created some uneasiness among the ladies sitting in the front pews and I took note of their reactions to prepare a future sermon about "equality before God."

After mass, Rosa came over to remind me about our dinner engagement. After assuring her that I would come by at the appointed hour, I returned to my room and continued transcribing the diary.

Around noon, my head throbbing with a migraine, I bowed to Juanita's pleas and took a two-hour break. As I ate, Juanita insisted that I not go to Rosa's home. Thinking she had been spying on me, I became angry.

"How did you know I would be at Rosa's tonight?" I demanded to know.

"It is the talk of the town, Father," she said, staring at the floor.

Rosa, who wasn't older than forty-five, was an attractive single woman. From what little I'd heard of her, she had been living alone since her husband died mysteriously two years before. In a small town like this, such facts were sufficient to set gossip in motion. I decided to go anyway.

It was just past sunset when I arrived at Rosa's home. There was a light in the window. As I knocked at the door, I noticed two figures moving on the other side of the street. My suspicion that I was under surveillance was allayed when I remembered that in small towns such as these, lovers often meet under the cover of darkness.

Rosa answered the door and led me into a tiny living room where she told me to make myself comfortable while she set up the table. I spent the time looking at the many photographs on every wall of the room. Most of them were of a man I supposed had been her husband.

She must have loved him deeply, for the photos spanned his whole life.

"Dinner is ready, Father," I heard Rosa say suddenly behind me.

"I was looking at the photos of your husband," I said like a child caught in mischief.

"And my son," she replied.

"Your son?"

"They were almost identical, Father."

"I knew your husband had died, but I didn't know you had a son."

There was silence. Rosa's eyes were flooded with tears.

"They took them both away from me. They killed them both, Father."

I didn't ask who "they" were. I knew. I took her by the arm and helped her to one of the two raggedy rocking chairs that were all the furniture in the humble room.

"Do you want to talk about it?"

"The food, Father."

Rosa told me that shortly after her husband had died in an accident while leaving the office of the union for which he worked, a jeep with three men inside parked in front of the house. Two of them got out and indentified themselves as being from the Army.

When she opened the door, they beat her to the ground and went straight to her son's bedroom. They dragged him out without a word, handcuffed him and then threw him into the back of a jeep. For the next two months, Rosa went to every government office she could, trying to get information, but all she got were lies. Then she heard nothing until an officer notified her, through Father Ramiro, that her son had died in a confrontation with the security forces.

Supposedly killed in that same incident was the younger son of Maria Arce, the woman I had seen in church with Rosa. Maria never saw the boy's body.

"What did Father Ramiro do during those two months?" I heard myself ask without being really aware of the motive behind my question.

45

"What else could he do, with his old age and arthritis, but to get us an interview with Bishop Ovando?"

"Bishop Ovando?" I repeated incredulously. I waited for more facts but Rosa remained silent.

"What did Bishop Ovando say to both of you?"

Rosa stared at me.

"Father, please do not judge what I am about to tell you as a lack or loss of faith on my part. You are different. I know you are different or you would not have said what you did in front of them during yesterday's mass."

"What did Bishop Ovando say?" I repeated gently.

"If you had learned to raise your children under the Christian principles taught by the Church, today you would still have them at your side."

"That can't be true," I interrupted.

"Yes Father, that is what he said. That is exactly what he said," she muttered.

We ate nothing at dinner.

Before leaving, Rosa made me promise I would come back to dinner soon. I said anytime and that made her happy.

About a block away from Rosa's house, I started to cry. For the rest of the night I locked myself in my room, and the first light of dawn found me working on the following entries:

CHAPTER XIII

February 9

I recognized the familiar stretch of the corridor, the sound of glassware and the same odors. Now I understand how blind people refine their other senses.

The first thing I saw when they removed my hood was the woman called Luisa. She was strapped to a bed, a cast on her left leg and a makeshift bandage around her head. Near the wall was the man who had been tortured in the water tank the previous day. He was naked and his hands had been bound to the same shackles he was wearing on his ankles, forcing him into a fetal position. I was strapped to another bed. The lieutenant asked the man about an attack on a particular army base. When the man didn't answer, the lieutenant began to call out several names. The prisoner remained slient. The lieutenant became impatient. As he pronounced each name he kicked the prisoner all over his body. He obtained nothing but groans and left.

After a short while, the lieutenant returned. In one hand he carried a motor oil can open at one end and in the other hand he held a paper bag. I heard strange squeaks and scratching coming from the bag.

The lieutenant was accompanied by a man I had never seen before who was carrying a blow torch and a fine metal rod about eighteen inches long.

Those who were torturing me obviously knew the purpose

of the items being brought because they immediately joined the lieutenant and became as children with new toys. They went over to the prisoner and carried him to the center bed. With ropes and chains, he was bound to the bed so tightly that his back arched.

"Now I know you'll talk, you son of a bitch," muttered the lieutenant while drilling a small hole through the bottom of the can. The other man handed him the metal rod which the lieutenant tested to see if it would go easily through the opening.

He then placed the opening of the paper bag over the open end of the can, and I realized in terror what had been in the bag—a rat that scuttled into the can.

The hairs of my body stood on end; I trembled. The lieutenant placed the open end of the can against the man's anus, using broad strips of adhesive tape to hold it in place.

I shook at the sound of the rodent clawing against the interior of the container and squeaking furiously and loud. Desperation was clearly marked on the man's face as he writhed violently.

"Talk, you son of a whore. Where is your leader?"

"Who the fuck planned the attack?"

The man groaned a couple of times but didn't say a word.

The lieutenant gave a signal to the man who came with him, who struck a match and lit the blow torch. After adjusting the flame, he slowly heated the metal rod until it became red hot at the tip. He gave it to the lieutenant who walked to the prisoner and carefully inserted it into the bottom of the can.

The intense heat made the rat go mad; its scratching became wilder as it searched frantically for a way out.

The prisoner began to scream for the first time since he had been under torture and to writhe so violently as to scare the rat even more.

Luisa was shrieking. I was beside myself. The torturers

48

turned up the volume of a radio and continued to watch the man's convulsions, mesmerized by his suffering.

Three times the lieutenant heated the rod. Luisa fainted. The man became motionless. I realized that the rat had suffocated inside the man's intestines. The horror drove me into unconsciousness . . .

When I awoke I turned immediately toward the center bed. The man's body was still there. There was a streak of blackish blood in the crack of his buttocks, around which were the rabid toothmarks of the rat, whose hairless tail protruded from his anus.

"Kill me!" I began screaming in rage.

From the other bed, Luisa burst into the frenzied laughter of the insane.

"These fucking bitches, take them away!" shouted the lieutenant.

We were untied, dressed and hooded. Luisa was still laughing madly as we were shoved out the door.

"One moment!" yelled the lieutenant as we were going out the door. I heard him say in a low voice to one of the guards:

"Take the nut to paradise and the other to the same place."

That's how I learned Luisa was in the same complex as I. I concluded that paradise meant heaven and that Luisa had been sentenced to die.

When we went out, I heard Luisa being taken to another car which sped off. I began cursing and kicking any shape I could sense near me. I was beaten savagely and thrown inside another vehicle.

When we arrived, instead of taking me to the cell, they tore off my clothes and tied me to the post in the backyard.

One of them yanked so hard on my hair that my eyes watered.

"Now you are going to learn, you filthy nut," he shouted in anger.

February 10 to 12
The first hours I spent tied to the post were more or less bearable until the sun came up. They gave me nothing to eat during the first day, and all I had to drink was the perspiration running down my face to my lips. The next day, the same.

By now, I had blisters all over my body and I knew that the pains I was feeling were a mere prelude to what was to come. To keep from losing my mind I had to find a way to assuage my hunger. I began chewing on a piece of the hood I had sucked into my mouth.

I managed to eat out a circle of cloth about two inches in diameter, not only relieving my hunger but welcoming fresh air. There had been very few times in my life when I had felt such satisfaction. I was so proud of my ingenuity that I felt a new will to live. I began to think of a way to quench my thirst.

The idea of crying to sip my own tears occurred to me but now I was too happy to cry. It seems that my suffering is soothed when I succumb to the absurdity of my circumstances. I feel almost at peace. In the solitude of my cell I reached the conclusion that when I refuse to accept this absurdity I suffer the most.

But now I am happy. I will not allow myself any form of depression. After sunset, a cool breeze kissed my naked body as if to add to my absurd contentment. The sound of the puppy made me forget my thirst and I listened intently. The sound was getting louder and a warmth was settling throughout my body.

"Rulito . . . Rulito," I muttered.

The puppy stopped its whimpering and I felt him licking my legs like Rulito used to. "Rulito, Rulito," I whispered again, unable to hold my tears. I sipped each and every one of them. I wanted to see him, I wanted to touch him but Rulito now wandered far away from me.

I tried to peep through the hole I had chewed in the hood. I leaned back my head and managed to see a small area of the yard. I recoiled in horror. There, under the moonlight, I saw an undernourished child staring at me from the ground, with wide eyes and an indescribable yearning for love.

CHAPTER XIV

By dawn I was still working on the diary. I felt it would be silly to try to sleep the remaining hour before seven. I convinced myself that after mass I would be able to catch a nap.

I left my room and fixed the strongest coffee I could tolerate. Besides being tired, I wasn't feeling very well and it showed. Juanita looked at me in alarm as she entered the kitchen.

"Are you sick, Father?"

"Sit down," I replied, ignoring her question. She looked like she was going to cry.

"I don't want anything to happen to you, Father," she said sobbing.

"Why should anything happen to me?"

"If they see you with Rosa they won't leave you alone, Father."

"They . . . who are they?" I was surprised to find myself asking the same question Susana had asked the building superintendent when her apartment had been ransacked by the militia.

"You know . . . them, Father, . . . I mean . . ."

"I know, I know." I got up and went to say mass.

As soon as I was through, I went to see Dr. Ortiz.

"I thought you were the best friend I had in town," I said to him sincerely but in exasperation. He must have been expecting that sort of remark from me, for he didn't ask for any clarification.

"And I wish I could continue to be, Father, but there are matters which would be better forgotten."

"Could you have forgotten them if, instead of Rosa's or Maria Arce's sons, it had been yours?"

He didn't answer.

"Well?" I insisted. For a moment, Dr. Ortiz stared at me with an almost defiant look.

"Father Ramiro forgot them . . . even the Bishop forgot them," he answered calmly.

I turned around and without another word I left. I walked slowly back to the church, feeling ill.

When I entered my room I took a long look around at the mess of paper strips. I was restless; I couldn't lie down. I suddenly remembered my dinner engagement with the municipal chief. I looked at the clock and went right back to work.

By three o'clock in the morning, I had read the following:

CHAPTER XV

February 13

I recognized the pervert when he asked his companion for a cigarette, but today he didn't engage in his customary indecencies. I am afraid I won't be able to withstand the howling of the child (or is it a dog?) any longer.

That night shortly before they came for me I heard the door to the adjoining cell being opened and a body being dragged through the corridor. That was the cell in which I had twice seen the kind eyes. I imagined the woman smiling at her tormentor. Soon, it was my turn. I was taken to a jeep and driven once again somewhere. During the ride I lay atop another body. When we arrived at the destination, they removed our hoods; my fellow traveler had been the woman with the kind look and the perpetual smile. Right away they stripped us and tied us to the beds. They began questioning me. This time, not only did they ask me about Silvia and her boyfriend, but they mentioned other names as well. One of the torturers brought up the notorious case of a general who had been assassinated by terrorists three months earlier. All I knew was what I had seen on television or read in the newspapers. I told them as much but that was pointless. They began applying the *picana* to my eyes, gums and genitals.

"The truth, we want the truth!" one of them kept shouting at me.

This "session" lasted for about half an hour and when they realized that I was on the verge of fainting, they left me and went over to the other woman.

She observed their arrangements for her with that blissful smile. She watched the torturer as he attached the electrical wire to her toe. One of the torturers put a cigarette out on her nipple.

She was shocked and punched all over as they asked her about the mothers of some "disappeared" who had taken refuge in a downtown church after being dispersed by security forces. From the few answers she gave, I noticed that she had a slight foreign accent. Just then the lieutenant walked in, silently observed the proceedings and left abruptly.

Two of the torturers took turns ravaging the woman.

For the first time, the woman stopped smiling. Her life was fading. Her face was now milky white.

They put the hoods over our heads to send us back. I could hear her being dragged to the car.

February 14
The woman with the smiling face died this afternoon. Through the window, I saw the lieutenant chop off her hands with an ax. I saw her spread-eagled on the ground near the post. Her wrists and ankles were tied to four stakes. She had blisters all over her body and was turning her head from side to side in an apparent effort to avoid the scorching sun. When she looked my way, I saw again that she was smiling. I fell to my knees and prayed for her.

I don't know how long I knelt there. When I went back to the window, the woman's body was in rigor mortis and the lieutenant was mutilating it with an ax while two men looked on. He chopped her hands off.

I crouched near the drain and with a single swipe, I caught three flies and, hurrying over to the spider's web, offered them in a ritual sacrifice. I shuttled between the drain and the web, talking to myself, until two guards entered the cell and strapped me to the cot.

As soon as I became lucid again, I heard myself say:

"If they do these things unto the green tree, what wouldn't they do unto the dry one?"

"This one is already cracked," said one of the guards.

"If they can do these things unto the green tree, what wouldn't they do unto the parched one?" I repeated. "Because if they can do these things . . ."

CHAPTER XVI

Last night I had a terrifying nightmare. It wasn't my run-of-the-mill nightmare—horrifying images, fire of eternal torment, snouted beasts. This time I saw the face of Jesus, smiling affably at me from behind bars and inviting me with his arms to come closer to Him. But when I approached He would back away until I could hardly distinguish Him in the depths of the long, narrow cell.

This went on for quite some time until I began to cry, and then Jesus started to come to me, very slowly. I felt at that moment as if I were floating in the midst of an aura; my body was relaxed, overcome by a strange sensation of happiness. Jesus came nearer and nearer as if in slow motion.

When He came close to the iron bars, I extended both hands to offer him a small figure molded of tripe as a token of my faith. Jesus reached for it and at that moment His hands became two bloody stumps covered with dirt. I woke up screaming.

When I woke up in the morning I was seized by hatred for Susana. This had happened before, but never with this much intensity. I am troubled by the suspicion that I am slipping away from the values of the church.

This morning I wondered whether I would have to stop transcribing the diary. For a moment I felt I had to make a choice between betraying Susana or my church.

I am so confused. My destiny feels as one of everlasting solitude.

Today at mass, I noticed the police captain flanked by two new grim faces. Rosa, whom I visit every other day, told me that the men had recently arrived in town, and everybody was quietly speculating that they were federal agents.

This was worrisome, so I decided to find out a little more about the matter. Later that night, as I strolled around the plaza in front of the church, I spotted the two forms that had followed me to Rosa's house. I returned to my room with the dignity that my fear would allow, trying to convince myself that there was nothing to be afraid of.

I prayed that I would have enough time to finish the diary that had destroyed any piece of mind that I could have had. I decided to do all work on the diary in duplicate and give a copy to Rosa, or Maria Arce, who joined us regularly. I felt that I could trust these mothers of children lost to the forces of repression.

That night, I worked very late and, before falling asleep, I had transcribed the following:

CHAPTER XVII

February 15

By the sound of their steps I guessed there were four of them. They pulled me through the corridor and out into the courtyard where I was tied to the post. The soft, fresh breeze suggested that it was early morning.

Soon, the sun began to burn like fire. I heard the by now familiar voice of the lieutenant.

"Bring her closer," he said. Then I heard moans and the steps of several persons as they neared the post.

"You know her?" asked the lieutenant. I heard a gargling sound. "Take the hood off her," he instructed.

As I blinked, trying to get used to the sudden light, the lieutenant asked again:

"Do you know her?"

Standing before me was Silvia, or what was left of Silvia. She was staring at me so insanely that I was sure she couldn't see me. Her body bore the marks of brutal punishment and she looked as if her skin was about to give way to her bones. Her eyes and lips were encircled by ulcerous sores. Around her nipples were pustules from cigarette burns.

"How about you, do you know her?" the lieutenant asked me. I exploded in shouts, crying as if I had gone mad. The lieutenant slapped me repeatedly to shut me up but I continued to scream uncontrollably.

"Take her away!" shouted the lieutenant impatiently.

They tied me to the bed and covered my mouth with adhesive tape. The image of Silvia was fixed in my mind and all the resentment I had felt for her gave way to compassion.

At dusk, the guard who usually untied me came on duty. He had always looked at me with kindness but never spoke. Now, however, he made me promise not to shout if he removed the adhesive tape.

As soon as he left I went to the window. It was already dark. Silvia's body, tied to stakes, looked very pale under the moonlight. There two men were struggling to keep two German shepherds on leashes away from the body. But this only excited the animals more.

I couldn't look any longer. I tiptoed to the drain and back again to the spider web. There were no more flies. I paced until I heard the dogs fighting between themselves. Imagining the worst, I cried, "Sons of bitches . . . sons of bitches . . . sons of bitches!" I covered my ears with all my might.

February 16
Today, surprisingly, they gave me a small piece of meat along with the usual insipid broth with noodles. The guard who seldom speaks brought me an apple. I couldn't eat the meat but I ate the apple ever so slowly, savoring every bite.

My stomach had become unaccustomed to such feasts; I was racked by violent cramps.

Time passed and I heard my cell door open. Three guards came in. I was stripped and then dressed again in another set of clothing.

"So bones is leaving us," one of the guards remarked. The others laughed.

I had noted the abnormal slimming of my shoulders and hips but it took the guard's remarks to make me think about how much longer I had to live. I was by then beginning to feel pain all over my body.

The guards led me to a vehicle and, I assumed, they would

take me back to the torture house. The few sounds I could identify from the floor of the vehicle were not all that familiar to me and as soon as I realized that the ride was longer than usual I began to fear that "bones is leaving us" meant that I had little time left in this world. I was not prepared for death. I began sobbing unceasingly. The trip must have lasted about three or four hours. Finally, I heard a voice yell, "Halt," and we came to a stop at what I supposed was a guardhouse.

A guard in the front seat got out of the car and returned promptly. We soon drove on and about five minutes later stopped again. Two men took me out of the car and I sensed that I was in the country; there was a quiet around me and I heard a dog bark in the distance.

I was ushered along a gravel path and taken through a corridor. I was forced to enter a room that I sensed was rather small.

I was strapped onto a bed covered with a thin, quilted fabric. The guards left. I was so relieved that I was not going to be killed. I fell asleep.

CHAPTER XVIII

The entries pertaining to just one date were becoming longer, and I had to search through more and more scraps of paper to find them. I attribute this to the fact that those days were clearer in Susana's mind because they were most recent.

My own condition is worsening. I am suffering from malnutrition; I feel weak.

Last Thursday I fainted during mass. Apparently, the first ones to come to my aid were the police captain and the two federal agents. Fortunately, I came to just as they were about to carry me to my room.

This had made me realize that I have to be more careful with my health and with the diary.

Today, I received another letter from Bishop Ovando demanding that I immediately come to the city to talk. I also got a letter from Bishop Antonelli cheering me up by his confidence that I must have good reason to keep Bishop Ovando "a bit worried." I don't feel I can continue to postpone the interview.

I finally decided to go by bus next Monday. Before leaving I will put all the scraps of the diary in their original box and take them over to Rosa's. Restoring their order will be a monumental task, but I don't know what else to do. Last night I made a greater effort and accomplished the following:

CHAPTER XIX

February 17

I heard my door being unlocked and someone approaching my bed.

"And this one?" a voice asked.

"They brought her in last night."

"Take her with the others," directed the first voice.

When they freed me and removed my hood I was in a cell a little smaller than the previous one with walls a freshly painted lime green. A window was covered from the outside with a rectangular piece of cardboard.

There were three men around me. The one who had ordered me untied was dressed in an elegant suit, while the other two wore military fatigues. I was stripped and handcuffed, while the man in civilian clothes watched indifferently.

"To the yard," he said to me as if I knew what he was talking about.

I didn't budge, and the other two shoved me out the door. We walked along a narrow corridor which was flanked by cells similar to mine. At the end of the corridor was an office with an enormous glass window facing the hall and to the right a door ajar leading to what looked like a bathroom. To the left was a shorter corridor.

The guards pushed me in that direction and we exited into a courtyard enclosed by concrete walls about ten feet high and topped by six strands of barbed wire. Facing one of the walls were several naked men and women. Some fifty feet behind them stood four soldiers bearing handguns. I was placed between a man absurdly thin and tall who was fighting to keep himself from falling, and the woman Luisa, whose leg had been fractured while she was tortured and who had lain beside me during the episode with the rat. I couldn't believe how happy I was to see her alive. The last time I had seen her I thought the lieutenant had sentenced her to death when he ordered his men to send her to "paradise." I, too, must now be in the place they call "paradise."

Luisa looked at me out of the corner of her eye and I could sense that she was also happy to see me. Quickly, she again fixed her eyes on the wall to prevent discovery of our connection. Suddenly the soldiers opened fire and bullets zinged all around us. The incredibly thin man fell, drenched in blood, to the ground.

I realized that the soldiers' intentions had not been to kill us but rather to scare us, but the thin man had been having trouble with his balance. One of the bullets pierced his head.

Moments later, I heard the soldiers protesting to the man in civilian clothes that their shots had not killed the prisoner. Several pairs of boot heels clicked, and another soldier emphatically stated:

"Neither did mine, Colonel."

"It doesn't matter, we have one fewer terrorist to worry about," the elegantly dressed man commented.

We were all returned to our cells at once. Luisa was in the cell in front of mine.

They didn't tie me down or put a hood on me, so as soon as they left my cell I put on my clothes which were on the floor. I then tiptoed to the window and peered through a tiny hole in the cardboard. I could see the same courtyard I'd been in. The thin man's body had not been removed.

February 20

Everything here is better. Somehow I suspect Silvia's death has a lot to do with it and that makes me feel quite bitter.

I have been fed far more regularly than I was at the other prison. The guards don't seem to be as inhuman and vicious. One of them allowed me to wash my face and I feel he would have even permitted me to wash my body, but he stood there watching me naked and I felt ashamed.

My feeling has been rising. I am holding on to some hope.

Through the hole in the cardboard covering my window, I noticed Luisa wearing the permanent smile of an idiot, chasing invisible flies around her or scratching her head as if she harbored a colony of lice there. The guards interpret her behavior as passive insanity, let her talk freely to other prisoners and walk around uncuffed. Yet, I am certain that Luisa is saner than her captors. I have seen her exchanging words with a dark-skinned captive sporting a partially singed mustache.

I've also seen Luisa talking to Alicia, the pregnant woman the lieutenant had spared from a *picana* ordeal, whose extraordinary beauty had startled me at the torture house. I would even swear that I had seen Luisa, after making sure no guard could see her, passing something to Alicia.

Today they left the peephole in my door open and I noticed that Luisa's cell door had no padlock on it. She was pushing a broom up and down the corridor and mumbling unintelligibly.

I was absorbed by Luisa's movements until I heard footsteps that were not hers. I backed away from the peephole, just in time to avoid being seen by someone who closed it. I was sitting on my bed when the peephole was opened briefly and a wad of paper was thrown in, rolling almost to my feet.

I unfolded it carefully. The words, "Bravery and Courage" were written on it.

The world seemed so marvelous to me that I began to weep. I read it and reread it a hundred times. Before the next guard shift I rolled the paper back into a small wad, chewed it thoroughly and swallowed it.

CHAPTER XX

The trip to town lasted well over the usual six hours because the rickety bus had carburetor problems and a flat tire. When I finally arrived in the city it was already mid-afternoon, and I rushed to the cathedral to get my meeting with Bishop Ovando over with, to be scolded and catch the 7:00 P.M. bus for the return trip.

Bishop Ovando was as anxious as I to clarify matters and didn't make me wait. One of his virtues was that he didn't beat around the bush.

"You look sick," he said with warmth and sincerity.

"Never felt better in my life, Excellency," I lied.

"Father Antonio," he said without wasting any more time on my health, "things are not proceeding as they should at your parish."

"I must admit, Excellency, that certain contingencies compel me to limit my time evangelizing but everything should be back to normal soon."

"And what are those "contingencies," if I may ask?" he inquired with an inflection that did not precisely invite confidentiality.

I fought with my conscience, floundering between the loyalty I owed to a superior and my fear of his reaction if I told him the truth.

"There have been some disappearances in town," I blurted out.

He didn't even blink.

"And what has that to do with you?"

"Well," I answered, disturbed by the turn of the interview, *"I have deemed it evangelical to dedicate part of my time to soothe the anguish of some mothers."*

"That is not your function."

"I thought it was."

"The authorities in your town are not exactly delighted by your inquiries into the cases of those women's sons."

"I am doing nothing wrong, Excellency! I am only giving consolation to those families for the loss of their children."

"I am not questioning your pastoral vocation, but failing to maintain the best possible relations with people in power does not seem intelligent to me."

"Sometimes I think that we are only concerned with accommodating the government. But there have always been men of the Church who have questioned that stance."

"And are you one of them?"

"Our silence in the face of repression and murder is nothing we should be proud of."

"So I repeat, do you agree with those who think our Church has compromised itself?"

"Perhaps," I said. *"And priests who questioned injustice in the past were not branded subversives and murdered."* I had gone too far. The bishop rose, fighting to conceal his annoyance.

"Remember, Father Antonio, that there is one and only truth. Our opponents are the incarnation of evil and must be eliminated. After all, fighting evil is our sacred mission. The principles of those trying to implant atheistic ideologies are absolutes. But so are ours. To invigorate our Church we mustn't allow ourselves to be weakened with doubts. It is our unbroken certainty that has made ours an unassailable institution.

"That is not to say that I don't understand your feelings. I

65

know that the teaching of Jesus and the dubious mission of the armed forces are incompatibles, but we must admit that our own survival may depend on the people that most of us despise."

I looked at him, amazed at his bold statement.

"It is not easy to be concerned with our own survival when in front of us is unfolding the drama of a mother who has lost a child to the hands of murderers," I said.

"Your intercession can only increase the sorrow of those mothers."

I didn't buy his sincerity.

"Should I take it that you are forbidding me from dedicating to these mothers the time I feel they are entitled to?"

"No, Father, I am not forbidding that. But I am certainly demanding that you pay more attention to other persons who can help our evangelizing cause and the Church that harbors that cause."

"Namely, in this case, the municipal chief, his two federal agents, and the group of ladies and gentlemen who deem themselves Christians but look the other way not to see the rampant official massacring, just because it is not their children who are being kidnapped, tortured or murdered."

Bishop Ovando abandoned every effort to appear courteous. He stopped caressing the crucifix around his neck and stood right in front of me.

"Father Antonio," he said annoyed, "I recognize the plight of the 'disappeared' and the enormity of the murders that have been committed, but the situation has no solution we can offer. I shall give you more time to meditate on your troubles but I fear that if you do not come to a quick resolution, your health will be completely ruined."

"Your Excellency, it is not the health of my body that I care the most about, it is the well being of my soul that I intend to preserve."

Bishop Ovando slumped into his rocking chair. For a while

he stared at the ceiling, caressing the crucifix. A dense silence took over the room.

"Would you like to spend the night at the parish house?" he asked suddenly.

"I'd rather return on the seven o'clock bus," I said.

"Good luck," he answered, extending his hand for me to kiss the ring.

I rushed to the door. I heard him call, "Antonio." I stopped.

"Cowards also deserve forgiveness."

I didn't answer. I couldn't even if I had wanted to. I wasn't sure to whom the Bishop was referring.

My mind was on fire during the whole ride back. I was determined to speed up work on the diary. I was convinced that my interview with Bishop Ovando would be my last.

The run-down old bus pulled into my town at one o'clock in the morning. I woke up Rosa and took the box back to my room. By four-thirty that morning I concluded that I succeeded in deciphering half of the diary so far.

CHAPTER XXI

February 22

A guard took me to the bathroom and in the corridor I passed Alicia. She was so pregnant it seemed as if she would give birth any moment. She was talking to the guard escorting her and as she passed me she looked at me with a friendly smile.

The calm that followed was almost unbearable. I started

to think about my parents and Nestor. I fell into profound despair. I cried uncontrollably.

I've been experiencing nasty headaches and dizzy spells for several days. Twice I have lost my balance.

February 23

The peephole in my door was again opened briefly, and another wad of paper rolled across the floor of the cell. This time it was a small piece of foil paper like the kind found inside a pack of cigarettes. "Faith and Hope," read the same handwriting of the first note.

Immediately, I tiptoed to the door and placed my ear against it, expecting to hear Luisa's incoherent mutterings, or the sound of her leg dragging. I heard nothing.

I read the piece of paper time and again, as I had the previous one. I tore it into little pieces which I then shoved into the drain. I heard my door being unlocked. The guard I had seen with Alicia came in.

"Let's go," he said.

He took me to the courtyard without saying another word and directed me to sit on the ground next to Alicia and a woman with raw burns all along her legs. There were two other women and three men.

Luisa dragged her leg as she paced the yard, talking to herself and chasing invisible flies. Occasionally she would stand in front of us and make obscene gestures.

The guards laughed and Luisa rewarded them with a mad grin. Once, she came near our group and began dancing a combination of flamenco and rumba, grotesque because of her limp.

I turned away from this pathetic spectacle and looked into the beautiful eyes of Alicia. She moved a little closer to me and touched my hand into which she slipped a scrap of paper. "Put it into your vagina," she said. Luisa's act had been some kind of diversion.

Making sure that the guards were not looking at me, I did as I had been told. I was now impatient to get back to my cell. As soon as I was in and they closed the door, I read:

"I have a friend who is a guard whose son was saved by my husband, a doctor. We know that you are educated. You must write about all of this so others will know what is happening. We will make sure that what you write will see the light of day. Within a few days they will ease supervision over you and it may even be possible for us to talk. Strength and Courage."

I became aware of feeling alive. I read the words over and over. I was euphoric, emboldened by the very ideas of describing our plight.

CHAPTER XXII

I couldn't sleep at all last night and as the light of day cast shadows in my room, I got up and went to the kitchen to make some coffee. Juanita, asleep in the adjacent room, came out as soon as she heard the noises.

"Shall I fix some coffee for you, Father?" she offered, while opening a cabinet.

"Go back to bed," I said sternly.

Juanita recoiled in shock at my tone and silently left the kitchen. I heard her quietly sobbing in her room.

Slowly I began to get ready for seven o'clock mass, while trying to recall my interview with the bishop. It was useless. I could remember only fragments, and not all that clearly.

One thing I was sure of: During the return trip I had decided to follow some of his advice so he would leave me alone until I finished the diary. But now I could not remember what that advice was.

I was walking unsteadily through the narrow hallway that connected a small administrative office with the church when I began to feel dizzy. I leaned against a rickety desk until I regained some strength. At the pulpit, I made every effort to conceal my weakness.

During mass I saw the same old faces in the same old places. The prominent ladies and gentlemen in the first row, the captain flanked by his two federal agents and the police commissioner in the second row. Behind two rows of empty pews, were Rosa, Maria Arce and an ever-increasing group of people from the poor neighborhood. Up to the midpoint of the sermon everything seemed to be going fine, and as I spoke in general about sin, the commissioner and the federal agents looked pleased while the indigents in the back looked bored.

One of the agents leaned over to the captain and whispered something. The captain responded with a broad smile.

I could no longer control myself. I drew an analogy between Judas Iscariot and the despots who ruled by terror.

I described the torturers as "emotionally handicapped" and made references to the anguish of those whose loved ones had "disappeared." I ended by asking for a prayer on behalf of the "victims of repression." The people in the back gladly obliged me while those in the front knelt only when they saw the captain and the police commissioner kneel.

As I concluded mass, everyone seemed eager to leave. The captain was just about to reach the door when I called him. The two agents rushed to his side.

"Is the invitation to dinner still open?" I asked insolently. The three of them looked at each other in surprise.

"Whenever you wish," answered the captain, forcing a smile.

"Tomorrow at eight?"

"Of course!" he said.

He was about to add something but turned around and walked to the door.

"Captain!" I called after him again.

"Yes?"

"Would it be much of a burden for you to have these gentlemen pick me up?"

"Any particular reason?" he asked, amazed.

"I am afraid of being murdered," I answered smiling.

"I don't think there is any danger of that," the captain assured me in disgust.

"Well, then, I shall come by myself."

He went out and I returned to my room to remove my sotana. My mood was still unimproved. I worked on the diary till mid-morning and asked Juanita to prepare lunch for us, which made her very happy.

After lunch, I locked myself in the room and transcribed the events of February 24 and 25.

CHAPTER XXIII

February 24

Luisa was the first one I saw. She was limping badly and scratching her head with both hands. The same people were in the courtyard, except Alicia, who arrived shortly after in the company of the familiar guard. He didn't object to my helping Alicia to crouch—her huge belly was hampering her.

As soon as he saw her sit comfortably on the ground, he

went to join the other guards standing nearby. Alicia waited for Luisa to start her obscene performance. Then I saw her put one hand to her knee and cover it with her other hand.

From the hem of her dress she extracted the ink cartridge of a ballpoint pen. She slipped it to me and in a whisper told me to hide it in the hem of my skirt. Slowly I inserted it between two stitches. When I finished Alicia heaved a deep sigh of relief. We glanced at each other.

"Either Luisa or I will supply you with small pieces of paper," she whispered. "Write on them, and, when Luisa comes around sweeping, when the peephole is opened, throw the rolled-up paper out to the corridor. If Luisa doesn't open your peephole, somebody is around."

"What if she doesn't come around on a given day?"

"Hide it and when you come out to the courtyard, give it to me."

"Where?"

"Where what?"

"Where shall I hide it?"

Alicia looked amused at me and smiled. I understood.

"How will these pieces of paper be smuggled out of this prison?"

She smiled again but just then she noticed a guard approaching and didn't answer. When he walked away, I asked, "Where will the writing end up?"

Alicia looked at the guard who was always with her and hesitated a second.

"I can't tell you yet," she said.

"I have a right to know."

"Your notes will all be collected in one place and the first of us to be free will do with them whatever we decide later," explained Alicia, not giving me a straight answer.

At that moment, the guard approached again and stood over us. We didn't talk any further.

Back in the cell, I began to think about what had happened

in the courtyard. I felt a gnawing discomfort. Everything was becoming too easy. Was this a trap? That night, I devised a few tests for Alicia the next day.

February 25

All night I heard the opening of cell doors and people being dragged through the corridor. I did not sleep. Through the tiny hole in my window, I saw that it was already dawn.

They took me to the bathroom once, and hours later they fed me. In the corridor I saw Luisa pushing a broom, sweeping imaginary rubbish, but I didn't see Alicia.

That afternoon they took me again to the courtyard where I saw that now there were two more men, but not the woman with the lacerated legs. Alicia came out considerably later and her regular escort helped her sit by my side. She asked if I was sick, since I looked so grave.

"If it is possible for you to send notes out of here, why don't you write to your family?" I asked.

Alicia looked straight at me and became pale.

"They threatened to kill my unborn child if I did," she said as tears streamed down her cheeks. I was moved but made an effort not to allow myself to be convinced that easily.

"But Luisa or I could communicate with our relatives," I suggested.

"Luisa has nobody out there and you, you are still alive! Any chance you have of staying alive until you are released, if you are released, will depend on your family's not knowing where you are."

I said I didn't understand.

"If your family goes public with knowledge of your whereabouts, you would disappear or be "transferred." On the other hand if there's no trouble, after a couple of months, they might decide to dump you into the legal system, charging you with some crime or another."

"How is it you know as much as you do?"

Alicia looked at the guard again and didn't answer.

"What do you want me to write about?" I asked.

"About everything you have gone through and still have to endure."

"Has it been decided who the notes will be taken to by the first of us able to leave?"

"To Bishop Antonelli," she said.

"No. I want them to be taken to Father Antonio. It is my only condition."

Alicia looked inquisitively at me.

"Are you sure?"

"I am sure."

"And where is this Father Antonio?"

"I don't know, we'll have to find out."

"Through who?"

"Bishop Antonelli, I guess."

Alicia's eyes opened wide. She was about to say something when the guards came to take us back to our cells. That night I was confounded and more depressed than ever.

I tried to remember the . . .

CHAPTER XXIV

The February 25 entry was incomplete. I searched the room the entire morning for what was missing, but couldn't find it. I felt uneasy about this. I thought that it would turn up most unexpectedly. I couldn't force this development out of my mind.

That night, I went to see Dr. Ortiz. I needed some psychiatric books I had seen in his library. His cheerful welcome made me feel manipulative. He invited me into the living room and inquired about my health. After assuring him that I was feeling fine, I asked abruptly:

"What do you know about post-traumatic disorders in individuals who have suffered severe physical and emotional punishment?"

Dr. Ortiz looked at me as if I was referring to myself. Knowing through Rosa and Juanita that there was gossip in town about the priest being "sick," I wasn't surprised by his attitude.

"Not much," he said, "because I'm not a psychiatrist. I can recognize some symptoms, though."

"For example?"

"Well," he said trying not to upset me about what he thought was my own problem, "the patient shows basic symptoms and associated symptoms."

"Tell me the basic ones first," I said with a look that said I was ready for the worst.

"The problem is that since disorders occur only in response to severe physical or emotional stress, their prevalence can only be discussed in relation to a specific tension."

Clearly the doctor wanted to know my reasons for asking.

"Try to set aside your scientific and analytical mind and, in this case, please generalize for me," I asked him with a friendly smile.

The doctor gave a long look and sighed, realizing that the battle was lost.

"There is a classic post-traumatic syndrome which has been defined in relation to a great variety of stressful situations, such as those suffered by prisoners in concentration camps,

men in combat, and serious accidents, rapes and catastrophes, among others."

"And what are the symptoms?"

"The syndrome includes dreams and recurrent nightmares, anxiety, insomnia, lack of concentration, irritability, hypersensitivity, depression and other disorders."

"What are the related symptoms?"

"There are many," Dr. Ortiz said, "but among the most obvious are vertigo, headaches, emotional instability, nervousness."

Satisfied with what I'd heard, I stood up. Dr. Ortiz seemed disappointed.

"Was I of any help?" he asked.

"I think so."

As we reached the door he held me by the arm.

"Father, I would like to help."

"There is nothing to be done," I said.

Back in my own room I tried to resume work on the diary but I couldn't concentrate. I lay in bed staring at the ceiling, analyzing, in light of my conversation with Dr. Ortiz, what I had learned about Susana while reading her notes. At seven-thirty Juanita knocked on the door and reminded me I had to dine with the captain. I got up reluctantly and slowly walked the five blocks to the captain's house.

I had wanted to vent my indignation at the state of things in the country against one of those responsible. Now, however, I was overwhelmed by profound indifference. When I arrived, the captain and his wife were very courteous during supper. We chatted about various innocuous subjects, but while the captain's wife served coffee, I brought up the issue of torture.

"There is no reason not to talk about that, but remember we are not going to reach an understanding unless we put aside our own resentments," warned the captain.

"How do you know I am resentful if we have never talked before about the subject?"

"Haven't you been listening to your own sermons, Father?" the captain said smiling.

"I guess you never thought I was referring to you personally?" I ventured to see his reaction.

"I'll be honest, Father, at this point I don't care. I have learned to do my duty without holding grudges," he answered with sincerity.

"Is that why you haven't ordered retaliation against me?" I asked sarcastically.

"To tell you the truth, I don't know why I haven't," he said looking amused. *"I guess I take you as a well intentioned human being who happens to be confused by the overwhelming inhumanity of the events."*

"Your acknowledgment that we are facing some kind of collective bestiality surprises me."

"I didn't say that!" insisted the captain.

"You imply as much."

"But I didn't say that the events were unjustifiable."

"Are they?"

"You have to realize that in fighting for ideals one is sometimes forced to resort to the ugliness of violence," he said.

"To killing indiscriminately and torturing the innocent?" I said trying to control anger.

"Most of them are not as innocent as you might think. But in any case, the inhuman practice of torture is justifiable if its objective is to gather information that will lead to the eradication of atheistic dogma. As abhorrent as it might seem, sometimes we must take advantage of the propensity for hatred and cruelty of the torturers so as to achieve the ultimate goal of preserving our moral values," the captain said in a tone that left no doubt he was convinced that he was right. He continued:

"The torturers may be unattractive to you, but they are, unconsciously, ready to sacrifice their souls for what they believe is a good cause."

"You fall short of sanctifying the torturers," I said.

"They do what they do for the well being of their loved ones: their wives, their children. But also to preserve the exalted mission of the church you represent, Father."

"Don't do me any favors," I replied.

"Don't be too harsh, Father; those whom you call fanatics and 'emotionally handicapped' in your sermons are often the raw material used to shape a great nation's future," he said calmly.

"You are an intelligent man, captain. How is it then that you do not believe in the power of teaching?" I asked.

"We are dealing here with evil, Father, which can only be brought to reason through coercion. We cannot depend on the stuttering insecurity of a bunch of faultfinding intellectuals."

"But at least words do not kill."

"With all due respect, Father, some men of the Church exaggerate the effectiveness of persuasion. In dealing with the scourge of atheism words don't seem to get results. Coercion instead, if implacable, ends up being persuasive. Terror sometimes can become holy terror."

"How can the howls of pain of a defenseless woman who is brutally stripped of her dignity and submitted to the most cruel torture ever be justified?" I asked angrily.

I could no longer stand the naturalness with which the captain spoke. I felt a sharp pain in my chest. Although he kept referring to torturers in the third person, I was convinced that the man before me knew from practice what he was talking about. It was strange to see him lovingly hug his two children when they jumped on his lap for a good-night kiss. Seeing the tender look in his eyes, I was appalled by the absurdity *of it all. I was no longer interested in continuing our futile exchange.*

The captain walked me to the door and even tapped my shoulder in a farewell gesture.

"We shall be friends, Father. Very good friends," he said after making me promise that this would not be "the last supper."

I arrived home at a quarter after eleven and worked on the diary until four in the morning, but without the usual enthusiasm.

CHAPTER XXV

February 26

The first piece of paper that Luisa threw inside the cell this morning was the wrapping of a cigar. The second was a promotional flyer from a well known household goods store. I could write more on the flyer than on the wrapping, although on the latter I even used up the spaces between the "El Habano" logo.

When I finished writing I waited patiently for Luisa's signal and tossed the rolled papers back through the peephole. When I was taken to the courtyard that afternoon, it took only Alicia's look of satisfaction for me to know that the first messages had gone out. I felt as proud as I ever had.

March 2
Just before dusk, the peephole was opened twice and quite a few wads of paper rolled as usual across the floor. It was a happy day.

CHAPTER XXVI

It was Sunday. Right after mass I had to baptize the pharmacist's third daughter.

As the ceremony ended, the pharmacist made me promise I would attend the "little celebration" he was having that night at his house. I didn't find it proper to decline so I nodded yes and went back to my room to work on the diary.

I worked until 8:30 P.M., then I went to Rosa's house and stayed until 11:00 P.M. Back at the Parish House, I resumed work on the diary. When I looked up at the clock it was already two-thirty in the morning. I had forgotten all about the christening party.

I went out and ran almost the entire distance to the pharmacist's house. Upon arriving, I noticed the lights were out. As a matter of fact, all the lights of the houses along my way back to the church were out and there wasn't a soul on the street, except for the two shadows I had seen rising from a bench near the monument at the "plaza," who followed me all the way to the pharmacist's house and back.

As I entered the parish house, I made sure they knew I was aware of their presence. I raised my hand to my forehead in

the form of a courteous salute. The two shadows disappeared
behind the monument in the plaza.

CHAPTER XXVII

March 10

It has been eight days of intense emotional stress. I have
been capturing in writing every fact and occurrence since my
kidnapping that I can remember. I struggle to recall events
that I have driven deep into my subconscious.

At the beginning I thought we would have problems ob-
taining writing paper. But Luisa never failed to provide it.
Where she was able to get such a variety of form, texture
and color remains a mystery.

Today Alicia told me that we already had nearly a full box
of notes on the outside. I asked her to tell Luisa not to throw
so much paper inside my cell; I couldn't keep up. Caressing
her huge belly, Alicia remarked that maybe in a couple of
days, I would be writing about a birth behind bars. In these
past eight days I have noticed that the guards invariably
watch the male prisoners in the courtyard more closely, even
though there are more women present. Their ancestral *ma-
chismo* makes them assume men are more intelligent and,
therefore, more dangerous.

Writing these notes gives me a special satisfaction.

I am scared about my change of attitude toward men.

Up to the day I was kidnapped I didn't know about perversity among men. I had had only my father and Nestor to consider.

All my life my father had been the man to whom I ran for moral support. I regarded him as an invulnerable superman for whom anything was possible, yet, tender enough to wipe my tears and comfort me whenever I was in distress.

Nestor's love and devotion also made me think of men only in terms of strength, compassion and tenderness.

All the exposure to pain and misery he had had in medical school had not rendered Nestor insensitive to human suffering. I have often seen the deep sadness in his eyes at the look of an undernourished child.

But don't the men who torture, rape and sodomize us have children who look up to them? And I have seen the tender look in the eyes of one of my torturers as he talked about his daughter's poems while fondling my genitals. It terrifies me to imagine my father and Nestor being like these men, but I wonder if maybe they are.

March 11

They took us to the *patio* early today. Alicia and I were sitting close together, exchanging a few words when the guards weren't looking, when we saw Luisa, mounted on a broom, moving in front of us and giving us a military salute with four fingers stiffly extended. It was her way of letting us know the number of notes she had picked up. I covered my face with my open hand to indicate that I had thrown five balls of paper through the peephole. Luisa came by a second time and repeated her salute; her face became unusually pale. I covered my face again. And so did Alicia. This time we were hiding our anxiety. Alicia whispered that she thought that our being taken to the *patio* so early was a sign that something was wrong. Our hearts froze when the colonel and the lieutenant showed up unexpectedly with two men we had never seen before. They walked around slowly, stopped directly in front of the group of male prisoners, and looked each one straight in his eyes. They stared long and hard into the face of a skinny man wearing rimmed glasses who suffered them with heroic impassivity.

After a while they left, muttering among themselves.

March 12

The missing paper has not appeared. Today on the *patio* Luisa insisted she had picked up only four wads by scratching her head desperately with four fingers. Alicia and I intuitively decided not to sit close to each other. She is as scared as I am. I noticed that the man with rimmed glasses was no longer among the male prisoners.

March 13

They lined us against the wall and the two men who accompanied the colonel and the lieutenant handed each of us a small piece of paper and a pencil. Then, the colonel stepped forward.

"Write down the following!" he shouted.

My hands started shaking. My entire body trembled.

". . . last day I had seen F. A. and I tried to imagine his always reassuring smile," he dictated.

I thought I was going to faint.

My God! This was the ending of the February 25 entry.

March 14

All day I waited for Luisa to throw at least one piece of writing paper into the cell. When she hadn't by mid-afternoon, I became desperate. When they took me to the *patio* I didn't see Alicia. My heart pumped furiously. I tried to calm myself by bearing in mind that Alicia was usually brought out after me. My anxiety mounted when, as time went by, no Alicia.

83

Luisa wasn't there either. I remembered that when I was being led past her cell the padlock was still on the door.

Now, back in my cell, I noticed that Luisa's peephole, which faces mine, was open. I sat on my cot imagining the worst. I tried to remember what I had written on the missing note. I couldn't. I am frightened.

Last night, I heard noises in the corridor. I put my ear against the door. I could hear several voices and a few moans. I returned to the cot perspiring profusely and lay face down to cry. Sometime later, a key slipped into the padlock on my door; at that moment I urinated all over myself.

The guard who entered was the one who had always been with Alicia. He sensed my fear, for he told me to relax. He said he had only come to tell me on behalf of Alicia that she had already gone into labor and most probably the baby would be born that very night.

I had never spoken to the man before but I felt like hugging him. I managed to control the impulse and, instead, sat on the edge of my bed and thanked him. He patted me on the head.

As he was leaving, I dared to ask him what would become of Alicia and the child. He said the baby would remain with the mother until such time as she decided where it should go. He added that normally the children end up in the care of their grandparents.

I was so excited at the turn things had taken that it took me some time before I noticed that the guard had left the peephole of my door open. I took a peek and I saw Luisa's eyes in her cell across the corridor.

CHAPTER XXVIII

Now I knew what had happened to the missing part of the entry of February 25. That mystery had haunted me ever since I had realized the entry was incomplete.

Last night I had another nightmare, but strangely I can't remember it as clearly as the others. It has left me physically wasted and this morning I feared I would not be able to remain on my feet during mass. But when I saw the looks of satisfaction on the faces of the captain, the police commissioner and the agents, I was emboldened and decided to preach along these lines:

"Political torture is imposed by those who have renounced their own humanity. A passage from Aristophanes' comedy The Frogs *seems to be the creed by which those amateur antichrists rule themselves. 'Bind him to the ladder,' wrote Aristophanes, 'string him up, flagellate him till bleeding, give him rope, pour vinegar down his nostrils, skin him, put roof tiles over his face, do everything unto him.'*

"And it seems that the last phrase 'do everything unto him' is the one that really sets in motion the imagination of these modern Tiberiuses because already they are going beyond the despicable practice of quaestio per tormenta. *Now the modern Tiberiuses, blood-gluttonous, find that the general practice of such human aberrations nourishes their repugnant craving for sadism.*

They torture in the name of justice, in the name of law and order, in the name of the country, and some go as far as pretending they torture in the name of God.

In remote ages, they tortured as a ritual. The ignorance or innocence involved in those tortures was perhaps the only justification that could redeem such barbarism, but could be the justification for torture now that man has already reached the moon? What reason could be found behind these atrocities except perversity, malice, treachery or sheer sadism?''

It was a long sermon and most of it was in about the same tenor. Once the mass was over, the people in the front rows left in a hurry, while Rosa Urquia, Maria Arce and the rest of the parishioners from the impoverished neighborhoods waited until the last of the others went out to start getting up.

I was in such a good mood that I went to the pharmacist's house to apologize for missing the christening party. While pretending to be extremely busy preparing a prescription he would every so often look out of the corner of his eye at the two federal agents who were on the other side of the street pretending to window shop at La Central store.

I went back to the parish house and worked on the diary until it was time to take the previous day's duplicates to Rosa, something I had been doing on a regular basis. Rosa told me that shortly after the morning services were over, the captain had taken off in his car toward the city and that she knew he hadn't returned, since she had spent all day watching the road that leads into the town's main street.

CHAPTER XXIX

March 15

This morning Luisa tossed two paper crimps into my cell, one the margin of a newspaper on which I'm writing, the other already filled by her with the following message:

> The guard told me Alicia's baby is gorgeous. But they never gave her the infant, since he had been promised to a captain of the Navy who had no children. The guard suggests we should tell Alicia there were last minute complications and the child died shortly after birth. The whole thing is horrible but I feel we should go along with him.
>
> It is Alicia whom we have to think of now and it would be far better for her to believe her child died, than to become another mother forever in search of a disappeared son.
>
> In case you have doubts about the guard, that he has been deceiving us and is also a traitor—consider this: The man is in a state because he suspects he too was used when he was instructed to give Alicia special treatment. He said he had welcomed the assignment, but that he would have given her the same treatment anyway because her husband once saved his son's life. And consider that he took great pains for almost a half hour to explain these things to me (you know I can only read

lips and I'm still not too skillful). We can trust him. Courage now is more important than ever.

As I read Luisa's note my heart was pounding. But I refused to cry.

March 16

I want to die.

I suspect that I am a despicable coward.

I was taken to the *patio* along with just a few others, including two new women who had black and blue contusions and patches of coagulated blood all over their arms and legs.

The colonel and the lieutenant were already there when we arrived.

Again they lined us against the wall. For a while the colonel walked with martial steps in front of us as if reviewing troops; then he stopped abruptly. Suddenly he flashed a piece of paper I recognized as part of the entry of February 25 and shouted:

"Who wrote this?"

Nobody answered. It was obvious that they had checked the handwriting against the pieces of paper they made us write three days ago. They went right to the man wearing rimmed glasses, and looking straight into his eyes the colonel repeated:

"Who wrote this?"

The man stared at him with contempt. The lieutenant slashed him across his face with the hilt of his whip, smashing the man's glasses. The man covered his face with both hands. I saw blood slipping through his fingers. The lieutenant asked again.

"Who wrote this?"

The man let his hands slowly slide apart just enough to spit saliva and blood into the lieutenant's face.

Two guards came running and knocked him to the ground.

The lieutenant waited for them to handcuff the man, while wiping off blood and saliva from his face. The colonel beat the man with his whip and kicked him all over his body with his pointed boots. I heard the sound of breaking bones.

I felt a compulsion to speak up. I swear I did. But I didn't.

March 17
All morning I tried to think about Alicia and Alicia's baby. But the man in rimmed glasses haunted me most of the time. And I think I was angry that Alicia and Luisa weren't sharing my guilt.

Whenever I was sure no one could see me, I spied through the tiny hole in the window. I saw the man with the rimmed glasses completely naked and bound to stakes stuck in the ground. Without glasses he seemed younger. He had bruises and cuts all over his body.

I have to talk to Alicia and Luisa. That man is going to die because of us. I have to make them understand. They don't seem to care. Don't you see? *They don't seem to care.*

March 18
Alicia was brought out but she didn't come to sit by me.

March 19
Alicia came to sit near me and all I could think of was to dissemble, to hold her hand. She looked emaciated but still beautiful. She started a conversation but didn't mention her baby. I told her about what had happened to the man. She trembled visibly. But she looked at me only as if to say there was nothing for her to do.

I told her that our silence was criminal, but instead of talking about the man she mumbled something about the lieutenant and spat with contempt on the ground. She was suffering the loss of her child so I didn't press her any further. She wanted to talk about the lieutenant. I told her I'd seen him chop off a woman's hands. She said that the woman was a Belgian nun who had been kidnapped for having dedicated herself to comforting the mothers of many who had disappeared.

She said that another general had been killed on the street in the capital city of another state and that the torturers would retaliate. For the first time I dared to ask if she belonged to any of the groups that were fighting against the government and she answered that her only sin had been to marry a doctor who wasn't an activist either, but an idealist who cured for free the indigents from the poverty-stricken neighborhoods. While she was telling me this I thought about Nestor.

I also asked her about Luisa and she expressed the suspicion that Luisa indeed belonged to one of the militant groups but she didn't know which one. In addition, she told me that, according to the guard, Luisa was to be released soon, for she had been labeled hopelessly insane. They hadn't been able to tie her to any extremist group.

CHAPTER XXX

Today, once again, I laced my preachings with open references to repression. The captain and one of the agents were absent from the audience. So was the pharmacist.

Around 10:00 A.M. Dr. Ortiz paid me a visit. I can't say I was all that disappointed. We sat facing each other across a worn-out desk in a tiny office and chatted for a while about the dispensary I had not been visiting these days as often as I used to. Dr. Ortiz watched me with great curiosity and I gave him the opportunity to talk about my health by inviting him to further elaborate on the disorders caused by severe emotional trauma.

"I already said I wanted to help," he remarked, "But I must know what this is all about."

"It is about someone who has suffered torture and humiliation to inconceivable extremes," I said.

His eyes opened wide in surprise and he sighed as if he had suddenly discovered a truth. I realized he still thought I was referring to myself and I let him believe it as much.

"I need to know more," he said.

"I've said all that I can," I answered, upset.

"I understand," he said. "That's a typical reaction."

Now I was the interested one.

"What do you mean?" I asked.

"The brain has mechanisms that block those experiences that cannot consciously be dealt with," he said.

"I remember everything," I said and he seemed disappointed.

"By definition," the doctor said, "the tension suffered must be severe enough to place itself beyond those human experiences considered normal."

"Is recuperation possible?" I asked.

"It depends."

"On what?"

"On the possibility of brain damage, for instance."

"Caused by what?"

"A regular subjection to electric shock, for instance." The doctor paused and looked straight into my eyes. "The picana, *for example."*

"What else?"

"There is a wide variety of personal factors which can determine an individual's predisposition toward developing pathological symptoms in response to trauma."

"Be more specific!"

"Age at the time of the startling experience, a previous mental condition; genetic propensities; the availability of social support are among those factors."

I was listening so intently I must have appeared absentminded.

"Father, how was one supposed to know that you . . ."

"Thank you, Dr. Ortiz," I said, getting up and reaching to shake his hand.

"Let me help you, Father," said Dr. Ortiz with such a pleading expression that I was moved.

"What is there for you to do?" I asked.

"Well, for now, I could prescribe something to arouse your appetite. Your weight loss is abnormal."

He didn't wait for me to say anything to write something down.

"Take one before going to bed," he said.

As he left, I noticed he had prescribed a well-known sleeping pill. That same afternoon I went to see Dr. Ortiz again, intending to thank him further for his concern but also to let him know he hadn't fooled me.

When I arrived, I found his wife crying and surrounded by several other women. She threw herself into my arms, sobbing uncontrollably.

"They took him away . . . they took him away," she cried.

Some of the women helped her to a chair while Rosa pulled me aside.

"They kidnapped her older son from the boarding house in the city where he lived with two other students."

"Where is the doctor?"

"He went to the city. He's acting crazy."

"When did this happen?"

"Three days ago, but they only found out about it an hour ago."

I stayed with Mrs. Ortiz and Rosa until midnight, then I went back to my room and worked on the diary until I fell asleep.

CHAPTER XXXI

March 20

Alicia wasn't mistaken about the reprisals for the general's assassination. There were no new incidents during the day but we were not taken out to the *patio*.

When night fell, there was the sound of cells being opened, groans, and bodies being dragged through the corridor. I imagined the skinny man bound to a cot or hanging from a hook. Worse yet, I imagined him with a can strapped to his buttocks. I cried in anguish. I must talk. But I want to live. I trembled with fear every time I heard a cell being opened but the hours went by and I was not taken out.

March 21

It was almost daybreak when they took me to a car. We made quite a long trip. I found nothing familiar, except the terror.

They took me out of the car and made me walk along a dirt path. I was sure the place was new to me. I heard a small metallic gate open, which I figured to be the entrance through a fence. We walked another few paces; I heard another door open; I was shoved into a place which I sensed was a small room.

"Take her to the operating room," I heard a familiar voice say.

They took me into another room and the same voice ordered that my hood be removed. The man speaking was the same man I'd seen in elegant street clothes who had ordered the soldiers to fire on us when we were naked against the *patio* walls. They had addressed him as colonel.

The room was the spacious living room of an old mansion. There were two metallic beds, a huge pail in the center of the floor, and a heavy chain with a hook suspended from where a chandelier must have hung. Close to one of the walls was the electrical control panel.

The men who brought me left, leaving behind the colonel and two men I had never seen before. I was stripped and tied to one of the metal beds. An electrical wire was connected to one of my toes. A pair of electrodes were attached to my temples. Alicia had told me that form of torture would force the mouth open and prevent the victim from screaming. Then, one of the men went to the control panel and the other grabbed the *picana*. The colonel approached my bed.

"Are you going to cooperate with me?" he asked.

I didn't answer. The colonel signalled the man with the *picana* who began to touch my nipples with it. I tried to scream but nothing came out.

"Are you going to cooperate?" the colonel repeated.

I said nothing. Again the colonel looked at the *picana* man.

"I'll be back in a couple of hours," he said and left.

The guard at the control panel left with him and came back with two others. I recognized one of them as having been among those who had tortured me at the other place and who had also raped me several times.

"The last time I saw her she wasn't too bad but now she's

a piece of shit!" he said to the others who burst out laughing.

"I'll fuck her anyway," said the one who had come with him.

"So will I," added the one with the *picana*.

"Well, hurry up before the colonel returns," advised the one who already knew me.

"No, we were only kidding," said the one with the electrical terminal. "This bag of bones is too disgusting." Everyone laughed.

From there on they tortured me without asking any questions. When the colonel returned he asked if I had said anything.

"Nothing," answered the one holding the *picana*. The colonel approached me again.

"What group does your boyfriend Nestor belong to?"

I was fainting.

"Where is the priest, Antonio?"

I lost consciousness. When I came to, I was on the floor of the car. I don't want to live any longer! . . . Lord, let it be the end!

CHAPTER XXXII

. . . I saw the soldiers tearing down the door and my father jumping the backyard fence. I ran after him yelling, "Daddy, Daddy!" and also tried to clear the fence. At that instant, I heard a volley of shots and my father fell over some thistle bushes on the other side of the fence. Between the planks of

the fence, I saw my father's bloody face. The soldiers who had broken down the door joined the ones who had been posted at the back of the house, and they all fired rounds into his lifeless body.

Then came a man wearing elegant street clothes who was addressed as "my colonel" and the soldiers moved to one side.

The colonel turned toward me and the sound of my weeping and approached the fence. I yelled, "Mama! . . . Mama! . . . Mama!"

I woke up screaming, "Mama! . . . Mama! . . ." There was a loud knocking on my door and I heard Juanita banging on my door and yelling, "Father! . . . Father! What's wrong, Father?"

CHAPTER XXXIII

March 22

The only thing that hasn't changed is the regularity with which Luisa keeps tossing blank paper crimps into my cell; I write on them and throw them back into the corridor. Otherwise, every day is different from the previous one.

There are people in the *patio* I have never seen before. Among them is a very young man. He could be an adult, but from the tiny hole in my window he looks like a child with his curly hair and big, dark eyes. He is very frail and can hardly stand up. The guards kick him every time they walk by and the man-child stares innocently at everything, as if he doesn't understand what is going on around him.

I don't know why the sight of that child made me think about my weakness, not physical but mental.

I spent much time thinking of the many forms of death. But what do I know about death? We never talk about death. It is not civilized. Only children speak openly about death. Children and torturers. I don't think I believe I can ever die, although as a Catholic I was taught about rewards in the afterlife. I want to live!

I thought about reincarnation and when one of the guards who came for me said, "There aren't many clients tonight for the operating room," I pictured myself wearing a surgeon's apron with a scalpel in my hand, plucking out the eyes of the lieutenant. I later regretted that, but at that moment I enjoyed the feeling of revenge. That was the worst part of it. Still, increasingly, I look forward to sweet feelings of revenge.

March 23

All night long I had been hearing much agitation in the corridor.

From my window I saw more than the usual number of people. Alicia was not among them but Luisa made the guards laugh more than ever by mounting the broom and riding among the prisoners while dragging her lame leg. Finally, one of the guards scolded her for creating too much of a ruckus. She howled like a coyote and began stamping her good leg like a little girl whose doll has been taken away. I didn't see the skinny man.

Around noon Luisa threw into the cell a message from Alicia and two paper crimps on which I wrote part of this. Alicia tells me that she knows what is happening to me; she has been reading my last writings. She said that Luisa is also reading them.

Late at night they came for me and took me to the torture

house. When the hood was removed, I saw that two additional metallic beds had been brought. Only one was occupied, by a woman about thirty years old whose skin showed the typical flabbiness of someone who has lost a great deal of weight in a very short time. Other than the two men working on the wall opposite the beds, everything seemed routine.

The men were cementing some metal rings into holes they had bored in the wall. They looked like common masons. Once in a while they would take a peek out of the corner of their eyes at the woman strapped to the bed. I didn't feel ashamed when they stripped me and bound me to the bed next to her, as these two brickmasons looked on.

Almost two hours elapsed with only the sounds of the masons working and hushed conversation among the torturers who were drinking wine at the other end of the room. Then in came the colonel. The torturers went over to meet him. He leisurely inspected the masons' work and I heard him say that he had met their wives and children and offered them his congratulations for having such wonderful families. He then dismissed them. The two men quickly picked up their tools and left.

The colonel approached the other woman's bed and asked her about a guerilla who had died six months before in the mountains of a province in the north. Then he asked me if I loved Nestor very much. I began to tremble. The colonel smiled and was about to ask something else when the door opened and two guards came in dragging a prisoner. They walked him to the empty bed and when they removed his hood it was the man-child I had seen on the *patio*.

From close up, I could see that he really was a child. The colonel asked who he was and why they had brought him in.

"He is a Jew," said one of the guards.

"Ah," said the colonel.

As they tied the child to the bed, the colonel watched the whole operation with little interest.

He watched the session for a while and then left. The torturers lost interest in us and went on with the child. They asked no questions but went about applying electrical charges to his circumcised penis while chanting "mother fucking Jew, clipped prick . . . clipped prick . . ." Then they beat him senseless.

When they too became bored, they brought us back to our cell in a van.

In the back, in a corner, the child was bleeding profusely from his nose and his mouth.

I knelt down in the darkness of my cell to pray for him and for the skinny man. Suddenly, I felt a sense of rebellion against all religious liturgies and against God Himself. Instead of praying I crept desperately around the cell looking for papers. I found part of a cigarette pack, and a piece of paper towel that to my shock already had writing on it.

I went to the window and held it up to the moonlight coming through the tiny hole and read it.

It was Luisa's handwriting:

I have been reading the notes for the past few days. I know what you are going through. I feel the same. So does Alicia. Desperation and guilt dull your senses like a drug. A nice feeling in a masochistic way. But we can't afford such luxuries.

Perhaps it will help you to think that even those who embrace an ideal in which extreme danger is involved, do so convinced that *they* are going to *survive*. Because *survival* is what it is all about. Because in clandestine prisons like this there are no rules except the rule of doing your best to *survive*.

I understand you. One day you want to die and next you want to live. That happens to everybody. But you finally will discover that the will to live is *always*, I repeat, *always* the stronger force.

So much for philosophy. Let's talk real life. If you talk, how long do you think it will take *them* to figure out who is involved? As a result, four people will die.

You think that if you had confessed to them that you are the author of the notes you would have saved a man's life. But nothing is farther from the truth. That man was doomed. We all are to a certain extent. But you or Alicia or myself may still have a chance. We are three.

Call it selfishness, in fact, call it what you want, but there is nothing heroic about this. You aren't trading your life for his, for here you do not own yours.

I know you won't disappoint me. You are a survivor. You want to live. So does Alicia. So do I.

I read the note twice. Little by little, I understood the words written by Luisa. I stared for a while at the door of my cell. It took on a new meaning.

I lay on the cot. Slowly, very slowly I chewed the ball of paper and swallowed it.

I felt relief.

I realized that my determination to survive was fueled by a powerful hatred.

It didn't seem to make any difference.

CHAPTER XXXIV

As I transcribed the entries for days twenty-two and twenty-three, I began suffering migraine headaches leaving me so exhausted that all I could do was to slip into a troubled sleep. The nightmare recurred. My father is killed, but now when I reach the kitchen screaming, it is Bishop Antonelli whom I meet. The bishop embraces me, and comforting me in a fatherly way, takes me to the shores of a lake. He produces a fishing rod, attaches a worm to the hook and for a while I contemplate the worm as it writhes, just before tossing it into the water. Almost immediately, the line becomes taut and I begin excitedly stamping my feet while pulling on the rod. The catch struggles so fiercely that I can't pull it in. It stops, as if at once all its energy had been depleted.

I pull the line in and, as it emerges from the water, I see a frail boy with curly hair and big dark eyes attached to the hook. He looks innocently at me. I turn to Bishop Antonelli for solace. He is no longer Bishop Antonelli but a man who speaks an unknown language. He hugs me almost to the point of suffocation. I struggle with all of my might to free myself, and run to the lake. But the lake disappears. It is a vast plain filled with rachitic children with big dark eyes who look at me with such innocence that I begin to cry.

I woke up in tears and couldn't sleep any longer. It was 5:00 A.M. I reread what I had transcribed that night and went over and over Susana's description of the masons and the

Jewish boy. Those two masons would never open their mouths to denounce what they had seen. Maybe they would tell their wives but no one else, for they knew that the wisest policy was to remain silent. Or maybe the masons would say nothing and their wives would never know that that night they had enjoyed the nakedness of another woman who was to be tortured. Those masons would not be concerned that sixty percent of the people who had "disappeared" in the country were workers like themselves.

Forgive me, Lord, but this world is shit!

CHAPTER XXXV

March 24

Upon arrival at the torture house, I saw a man strapped to a chair and one of the torturers pulling him back by the hair. Two blinding spotlights burned into his eyes. Between the two lights stood the colonel. He asked the man what *cuadros* he had. It was Alicia who told me that *cuadros* meant "contacts."

The man seemed to have been enduring the "third degree" for some time for he was perspiring profusely and his eyes were bloodshot. Every time his eyelids dropped, the guard behind him would yank his hair and force him to stare at the lights. I couldn't see him anymore after they finished undressing and strapping me to the bed, but I could still hear the questions about the *cuadros* he supposedly had, and about someone called Cornejo, whom they occasionally mentioned as the leader of a subversive organization.

About an hour had passed when I saw a distinguished looking man with a stethoscope hanging from his neck walk past my bed. Shortly after, I heard a body being dragged, the spotlights went out and the colonel now stood by my bed.

"I want to help you," he said softly. "But how can I help you if you won't help me to uncover the real enemies of our Christian nation?"

I don't know why, but I asked him what he wanted.

"A confession," he said, "only one confession and you would be rendering an enormous service to your country. And above all, you'd be regaining your liberty."

I was speechless.

"Think of your parents. Isn't it worth the life of your parents, the little cooperation I'm asking from you? Or the life of your boyfriend, Nestor."

My body went limp.

"No! . . . No! . . ." I screamed and began to cry.

The colonel tenderly wiped away my tears and patted me on the forehead as my father used to when comforting me.

"You'll tell me what organization Father Antonio belongs to, won't you?" he said.

I implored him with my eyes to believe me.

"To none. Truly, he doesn't belong to any."

The colonel signalled the torturer closest to me. He approached with the *picana* in hand.

"Shall I hit her?"

"No," said the colonel. "This seditious bitch deserves to be killed."

They untied me from the bed and placed me facing the furthest wall.

Twice the colonel asked me if I was ready to talk. Each time I heard the sharp blasts of a gun and debris from the wall splintered and pitched off my skin as the bullet crashed into the wall close to my head.

The last thing I remember is falling in a heap. I opened my eyes and I was on the floor of my cell. I didn't move for a while. I just stared at the ceiling, thinking of Mama . . . Papa . . . Nestor.

CHAPTER XXXVI

Dr. Ortiz came to see me this morning. Through Rosa, I learned he had gone to the city three times and was moving heaven and earth to learn about his son who had disappeared. As we sat opposite each other at my worn-out desk, his face looked pale and emaciated.

He said he had personally talked to the Commander of the Third Army and to a commissioner friend of his and that he had filed a stay of habeas corpus. He had even talked to Bishop Ovando.

"I feel, Father, I misjudged the bishop."

I didn't respond, and he went on to say that the bishop was a man very sensitive to these problems and that, judging by the concern he demonstrated, he thought he could count on his valuable assistance.

I'm not sure why I was compelled to ask him what the bishop had said. Maybe I was expecting the doctor to say something that would check the nausea I was beginning to feel.

"The bishop said that the steps I had already taken were

the right ones. He promised to talk to the chaplain of the Third Army. He suggested that I maintain a close relation with the municipal chief. In fact, he seemed to have the highest regard for the captain as a Christian and a soldier."

CHAPTER XXXVII

March 25

I no longer care what they do to me. When they mentioned my parents and Nestor, they smashed to bits the shield I had used to protect my soul. They have forced me to confront the idea of horror endured by those I love. I know that today they will come for me again. But I don't care. My parents are suffering. Nestor is suffering.

When they took me to the bathroom I passed by Luisa and I didn't care that I saw her. By mid-afternoon, through the tiny hole in my window, I saw Alicia among other prisoners in the *patio*. She appeared anxious, constantly checking the exit, waiting for me to come out. It didn't matter.

Later that night, they came for me. I was waiting. The trip was longer than that of the previous night but we went to the same place. It seemed longer because I was anxious to get there. I wanted to suffer. I had to suffer.

"Go ahead! . . . make me suffer . . . you sons of a bitch!"

They took off my clothes and bound me to the bed but didn't remove the hood. I heard them drag in another body and place it on the bed next to mine. I could hear the person gasping. The torturers started working me over. First they applied the *picana* from head to toe. Then they raped and sodomized me with something blunt and hard, and finally they beat me until I lost consciousness.

When I came to they had removed the hood. The first thing I heard was the choked sobbing of a man on the bed next to mine, repeating in a heartbreaking voice, "Susana . . . Susana . . . Susana."

I turned toward the man.

It was Nestor.

CHAPTER XXXVIII

There are only half a dozen diary entries left to be transcribed. Yet, I spent the entire day wandering between my room and the altar. Often I stared at the remaining notes but couldn't gather the courage to even touch them. For hours I prayed kneeling before the Lord, but I wasn't able to overcome my fear of discovering the outcome.

I walked in dizziness to the pharmacy. I visited Rosa and Dr. Ortiz. I headed for the poor neighborhood but my head-aches became so severe that I had to turn back.

I went back to Rosa's house and we had dinner with Maria Arce. I mentioned that I would be taking a few days' vacation.

Both said they would miss me but they were happy for me. They went on about my poor health and how much I had helped them to bear their misfortunes.

I returned to my room around 10:00 P.M. I lay in bed, staring at the notes to be transcribed.

. . . Before me, I saw soldiers tearing down the door and my father jumping the backyard fence. I ran after him yelling, "Daddy, Daddy!" as I, too, tried to clear the fence. At that instant, I heard a volley of shots and my father fell over some thistle bushes on the other side of the fence. Through a space between two planks of the fence, I saw the bloody face of my father. The soldiers who had broken down the door joined the ones that had been posted at the back of the house and shot him several times more.

Then came a man carrying a short-hilted whip, whom they called "the lieutenant," and the soldiers moved aside. At the sound of my weeping the lieutenant turned his face toward me. He approached the fence and I yelled, "Susana . . . Susana . . . Susana!" until my mind adjusted itself to reality. I looked at the clock—it was five minutes after three. I wiped my perspiration in the sheets and stared for some time at the papers.

I got up; I began the final descent into Susana's hell.

CHAPTER XXXIX

March 26

Nestor was already there. So was Alicia. The lieutenant appeared with four of his men.

Alicia was already bound to one of the metal beds. I was stripped of my clothes and strapped down to another. Nestor was on the floor, his hands and feet shackled.

The lieutenant ordered his men to leave the room and to stay out until he called them. As soon as the four men left, the lieutenant climbed on top of Alicia. She frantically searched for my eyes, imploring me to help her. I turned away from her. There is nothing I can do. Nothing I can do. It was all over very quickly.

The lieutenant called his men back and when they returned they hooked Nestor up. The lieutenant asked me about Father Antonio. I had no answer. He kicked Nestor and asked him the same question. Nestor seemed to be drugged. The lieutenant asked if he understood what they were going to do to him and he slurred badly as he answered yes. They raised him with the pulleys and submerged him head first into a huge vat of water. His body began to contort; the lieutenant ordered him pulled up and repeated his question about Father Antonio.

They submerged him again, pulled him out, and asked him about Father Antonio again. Once again, twice, three more times. He was motionless.

"Son of a bitch," I yelled, "you son of a bitch . . . he understands, Nestor always understands, you hear me, son of a bitch?"

CHAPTER XL

That was all. I searched all over the floor, even under the bed for more scraps of paper but there were none. The entry for March 26 became the last one in the diary.

The next two days were days of terrible confusion for me. I searched in vain for something to fill the emotional void left in me by the abrupt ending of the diary. I decided to write to Bishop Ovando, admitting that he was right about the deterioration of my health and asking him to send a replacement as soon as possible, for I was seriously ill. I had fallen into a bottomless depression.

During the week it took the new priest to arrive, I abandoned my daily routine. The only thing I did was visit Rosa, and each time I asked her to take good care of the manuscript. I also told her that it was not finished and that from the capital city I would be sending her whatever I could continue to write.

Dr. Ortiz became a source of conflict because, even though I felt the deepest sympathy for the disappearance of his son, it didn't match the profound sorrow I had shared with other parents whose children had also disappeared. I despised myself for feeling ambivalent about his loss because he had been among those who "looked the other way" until the scourge touched his own flesh.

I placed all the scraps of paper and the original manuscript in the same box in which they had been delivered to me and, along with a small valise, I left them in a corner of my room.

When the new priest arrived, I spent a whole day with him, explaining what had been done and what remained to be done. I recommended that he search out Rosa Urquia, Maria Arce and all the people from the poor neighborhoods, but he was not so inclined. He wore the most neatly ironed sotana I ever saw and as much as I tried I couldn't picture him walking in his shiny shoes through the dusty streets of the poor sector. I decided that those cold blue eyes had never seen pigs, chickens, dogs and children fighting for a wounded pigeon in the mud.

The next day Rosa, Maria Arce, Juanita and some other humble people came to say farewell to me. Juanita wept like Magdalena. And as the rundown bus turned the corner in front of the plaza, I saw the two federal agents leave the shade of the monument, and head toward the captain's house.

OMAR RIVABELLA

Arriving in the city, I went to Bishop Ovando to thank him for his understanding.

"Father Antonio," he said, "it is not I, but you who had to understand the circumstances in which we are living. Inasmuch as I do not approve of their method, at least I recognize that these people are doing something to eradicate ideologies that are harmful to the Church."

The Bishop seemed quite satisfied with himself and was in a talkative mood.

"You haven't made many friends in the town," he went on, "and you will not make many friends in other towns if people continue to fear you."

I really didn't owe this bishop anything.

That night I boarded the broken-down train that in two days would arrive in the capital, where the Patriarch Antonelli was awaiting me.

The train in which I rode was full of humble people fleeing the burning sun of the cotton fields to throw themselves into the industrial tumult of the twine mills.

They looked at me apprehensively from under the rims of their hats, thinking who knows what about the pale-faced priest who didn't utter a single word in two days and who clutched a cardboard box against his chest even when he fell asleep and his head banged against the window.

CHAPTER XLI

Monsignor Antonelli was shocked at my ghostly appearance.

"Antonio, you look like a phantom."

He insisted I see a doctor immediately. I told him I wouldn't see anyone until he listened to me.

We spent about two hours talking and he took another three to read the manuscript, sunk in a rocking chair at the far end of his office. I simply sat there.

Twice he was interrupted by his secretary and the third time he very courteously ordered him not to disturb him again until further notice. When he was through he fixed his eyes on me for quite a while.

"Let's have lunch," he said.

"It's already three o'clock, Excellency," I reminded him.

"So let's have lunch and dinner," he replied, calling his secretary to make the necessary arrangements right there in the office.

"You must recuperate. You shall stay sometime with Father Martin and Father Ernesto," he said, giving me a kind look.

That was not what I wanted to hear. What I wanted to know was what was he going to do with the manuscript.

"Everything, my dear Antonio," he said, "everything that is humanly possible."

He got up, put the manuscript in a vault and told me to take a nap in the rocking chair until he returned. He sensed

I was about to say something and in a soft but firm voice ordered me not to leave the office until he returned.

He came back after 10:00 P.M. *and handed me a pair of trousers and told me not to wear the* sotana *or the clerical collar for the time being.*

"Let's go," he said when I was ready.

We got into an old car and he drove across the city to a suburban district. We stopped in front of a parish house by an old church and there I met Father Martin and Father Ernesto. The Patriarch introduced them to me as "two of ours" and to them he said, "I place in your hands one of my sons."

He told them to force me to eat, if need be. He ordered me to rest and said he would come to see me within a week.

For the first three days Father Ernesto and Father Martin lavished me with attention and care, even though I woke them three or four times a night with my screaming.

Four days after I returned to the capital city, I was obsessed with the idea of visiting Susana's parents. Because Bishop Antonelli had prohibited me from doing anything that might be an emotional strain, it wasn't easy to convince Martin and Ernesto to let me go. But in the face of my stubbornness, they agreed, providing I returned by mid-afternoon.

Martin gave me directions to the sector of the city where Susana's parents lived. I had to take two buses and the last one left me about three blocks away from my destination.

I walked down a tree-lined street in a well-to-do residential area and stopped in front of the house, set in a garden surrounded by a fence. Weeds grew wild and the flower pots hadn't been tended in a long time. The place seemed abandoned and I wondered if Susana's parents had moved out. I found a doorbell near the paint-flaked gate, but after trying it for some time without anybody answering, I pushed the gate open enough to go through, and walked up to the front door. Two women neighbors curiously observed my movements from the other side of the street.

I knocked twice. Suddenly the door was partly opened and a disheveled white-haired head appeared. At first I didn't realize that the woman was Susana's mother. She looked at me for a moment.

"Father Antonio," she finally exclaimed as she opened the door wide and embraced me like a son she hadn't seen in a long time.

She led me to a chair in the living room. We sat next to each other, holding hands. There wasn't much left of the distinguished lady I used to know. She had lost weight beyond recognition and she seemed to have slept for weeks in the same wrinkled shirt she was wearing. Yet she was the one who asked:

"Are you sick, Father?"

"No, I'm perfectly alright."

We didn't know what to say to each other.

"And your husband?"

She raised her hands to cover her face and answered through her fingers:

"Sitting in his usual place."

"What place?"

"In the rocking chair, staring at the jar. Always staring at the jar."

I comforted her and felt an urge to cry. Poor thing, Susana's disappearance had been too much for her.

"We did everything, Father. Habeas corpus, we wrote letters to all the human rights organizations we could think of, ministers, bishops, even to the President himself."

She paused.

"And Nestor, Father. Nestor also disappeared."

I turned my face away from her. I said nothing. I didn't have the heart to say anything.

"Let's pray."

We knelt by the sofa and prayed. After a while I helped her up and asked to see her husband. She took me silently through a hallway to the rear of the house where, I remembered, the doctor had a small laboratory which he proudly showed me the last time I was there to bless the engagement of Susana and Nestor.

As she opened the door, I inhaled the stale odor of a room with no ventilation. The flasks and test tubes were covered with dust and the floor had obviously not been swept in quite some time.

The doctor was sitting in a rocking chair with his eyes fixed on a large jar. He didn't move when I stood by to greet him.

The jar commanding his attention was filled with a dark, bloody liquid. It contained something I couldn't make out at first.

"What is that?" I asked Susana's mother.

"Show him, show it to him," exclaimed the father, snapping out of his apathy before the woman could reply.

"No Eduardo, please no!" she implored.

I walked up to the shelf, took the jar and inspected it.

I became even more puzzled by the tinkling sound of something metallic hitting against the glass. I almost dropped the jar; I was about to retch.

Inside were two hands, severed at the wrists. One of them bore a ring on the middle finger. Together they floated in the bloody liquid, in a macabre ballet. There was Susana's engagement ring.

EPILOGUE

Mr. Omar Rivabella
New York, New York

Dear Mr. Rivabella,

Father Antonio had spoken to me quite often about you. He used to refer to you with a certain nostalgia as "that agnostic with a sense of humor, who used to say he respected me for my condition as a man, in spite of everything."

Anyway, after reading the enclosed manuscript you will know who I am.

Father Antonio is currently hospitalized at the National Institute of Mental Health, in the capital city of the Republic, where I am permitted to visit him once a week. It is with great sorrow that I must notify you that Sister Theresa, a nun who has him under her care, feels that the day is very near when the Lord will call Father Antonio by His side.

Father Martin and Father Ernesto have given me the details and circumstances which prompted his confinement in the Institute. They said that ever since he returned from the house of Susana's parents, Father Antonio would wake them at any hour of the night and shake them violently.

Father Antonio could not fall asleep.

They attributed the condition to the high fever he was

running all those days and they summoned a doctor. He prescribed only aspirin and rest.

That afternoon the fever broke and he became quite relaxed. They decided then not to keep from him any longer news that was two days old. Bishop Antonelli had died in a suspicious auto accident.

Fathers Martin and Ernesto say that upon learning this, Father Antonio burst into laughter and continued to laugh uncontrollably for several hours.

The doctor was called back and he suggested Father Antonio be brought to the Institute, where he is now.

I don't know if he is happy to see me because he looks at everything with no expression.

Sometimes he mutters words or names that only I can understand: they are from the manuscript.

During my last visit, while we were sitting on a bench at the Institute's courtyard, he seemed to recover his sanity. His face was full of so much life. He took my hands, just the way he used to when he comforted my sorrows, and pronounced some unintelligible words.

Then he pulled from his shirt pocket a piece of paper he seemed to have prepared for this last interview. He gave it to me and said in an enthusiastic tone, "To him, send it to him." On the piece of paper was your name and address.

With affection,
Rosa Urquia

FOR THE BEST IN PAPERBACKS, LOOK FOR THE 🐧

FOR THE BEST IN PAPERBACKS, LOOK FOR THE

KING PENGUIN

A Confederacy of Dunces   John Kennedy Toole

In this Pulitzer-Prize-winning novel, in the bulky figure of Ignatius J. Reilly, an immortal comic character is born. 'I succumbed, stunned and seduced . . . it is a masterwork of comedy' – *The New York Times*

The Labyrinth of Solitude   Octavio Paz

Nine remarkable essays by Mexico's finest living poet: 'A profound and original book . . . with Lowry's *Under the Volcano* and Eisenstein's *Que Viva Mexico!*, *The Labyrinth of Solitude* completes the trinity of master-works about the spirit of modern Mexico' – *Sunday Times*

Falconer   John Cheever

Ezekiel Farragut, fratricide with a heroin habit, comes to Falconer Correctional Facility. His freedom is enclosed, his view curtailed by iron bars. But he is a man, none the less, and the vice, misery and degradation of prison change a man . . .

The Memory of War and Children in Exile: (Poems 1968–83)   James Fenton

'James Fenton is a poet I find myself again and again wanting to praise' – *Listener*. 'His assemblages bring with them tragedy, comedy, love of the world's variety, and the sadness of its moral blight' – *Observer*

The Bloody Chamber   Angela Carter

In tales that glitter and haunt – strange nuggets from a writer whose wayward pen spills forth stylish, erotic, nightmarish jewels of prose – the old fairy stories live and breathe again, subtly altered, subtly changed.

Cannibalism and the Common Law   A. W. Brian Simpson

In 1884 Tod Dudley and Edwin Stephens were sentenced to death for killing their shipmate in order to eat him. A. W. Brian Simpson unfolds the story of this macabre case in 'a marvellous rangy, atmospheric, complicated book . . . an irresistible blend of sensation and scholarship' – Jonathan Raban in the *Sunday Times*

FOR THE BEST IN PAPERBACKS, LOOK FOR THE

KING PENGUIN

Bedbugs Clive Sinclair

'Wildly erotic and weirdly plotted, the subconscious erupting violently into everyday life . . . It is not for the squeamish or the lazy. His stories work you hard; tease and torment and shock you' – *Financial Times*

The Awakening of George Darroch Robin Jenkins

An eloquent and powerful story of personal and political upheaval, the one inextricably linked with the other, written by one of Scotland's finest novelists.

In Custody Anita Desai

Deven, a lecturer in a small town in Northern India, is resigned to a life of mediocrity and empty dreams. When asked to interview the greatest poet of Delhi, Deven discovers a new kind of dignity, both for himself and his dreams.

Collected Poems Geoffrey Hill

'Among our finest poets, Geoffrey Hill is at present the most European – in his Latinity, in his dramatization of the Christian condition, in his political intensity . . . The commanding note is unmistakable' – George Steiner in the *Sunday Times*

Parallel Lives Phyllis Rose

In this study of five famous Victorian marriages, including that of John Ruskin and Effie Gray, Phyllis Rose probes our inherited myths and assumptions to make us look again at what we expect from our marriages.

Lamb Bernard MacLaverty

In the Borstal run by Brother Benedict, boys are taught a little of God and a lot of fear. Michael Lamb, one of the brothers, runs away and takes a small boy with him. As the outside world closes in around them, Michael is forced to an uncompromising solution.

FOR THE BEST IN PAPERBACKS, LOOK FOR THE 🐧

KING PENGUIN

The Beans of Egypt, Maine Carolyn Chute

Out of the hidden heart of America comes *The Beans* – the uncompromising novel about poverty and of what life is like for people who have nothing left to them except their own pain, humiliation and rage. 'Disturbingly convincing' – *Observer*

Book of Laughter and Forgetting Milan Kundera

'A whirling dance of a book . . . a masterpiece full of angels, terror, ostriches and love . . . No question about it. The most important novel published in Britain this year' – Salman Rushdie in the *Sunday Times*

Something I've Been Meaning to Tell You Alice Munro

Thirteen brilliant and moving stories about women, men and love in its many disguises – pleasure, overwhelming gratitude, pain, jealousy and betrayal. The comedy is deft, agonizing and utterly delightful.

A Voice Through a Cloud Denton Welch

After sustaining a severe injury in an accident, Denton Welch wrote this moving account of his passage through a nightmare world. He vividly recreates the pain and desolation of illness and tells of his growing desire to live. 'It is, without doubt, a work of genius' – John Betjeman

In the Heart of the Country J. M. Coetze

In a web of reciprocal oppression in colonial South Africa, a white sheep farmer makes a bid for salvation in the arms of a black concubine, while his embittered daughter dreams of and executes a bloody revenge. Or does she?

Hugging the Shore John Updike

A collection of criticism, taken from eight years of reviewing, where John Updike also indulges his imagination in imaginary interviews, short fiction, humorous pieces and essays.